DARK LEGACY

A Raven Crawford Story

J. C. McKenzie

The gaping maw of the tunnel filled with wild magic stared back at Raven. If she had a choice, she'd hop right out of here. The erratic power licked at her skin like the blistering warmth from a campfire. Little pricks and sizzling snaps of heat followed by damp cold.

She turned to Cole. Maybe they could track the abductors another way.

He glanced down at her, face grim. "We have to go in."

"You swore you couldn't read my mind."

"Didn't need to."

She sighed and turned back to stare at the tunnel some more. Nope. Still freaky. She *knew* the troll passageway wasn't a living entity, not capable of conscious thought, but the air around the entrance vibrated as if Torghatten laughed at her.

Though she had troll guards standing behind her and her anam cara beside her, they did little to settle the unease flittering along her spine.

Mike whined and pressed against her leg. She'd prefer to pick him up and hold him tight, with his fur tickling her nose, but she needed her hands free. And realistically, Mike was better off on the ground. Quick and sly, he had a better chance of survival by ducking away and darting off into the sunset instead of being coddled by his older sister.

"Let's do this."

Standalone Titles

Cormorant Run

The Night House

The Good Griffin

Call of the Deep (The Shucker's Booktique)

Stormbound (Be My Love)

Conspiracy of Ravens
"Raven is my kind of people. Half hot-mess, half bad-ass, all awesome... the story had plenty of humor, action and mystery rolled up in a nice paced story."
~ Urban Fantasy Investigations

Nevermore
"The dramas, dangers, intrigue, and tension of *Nevermore* will have you glued to the pages, and when it is finished, Ms. McKenzie will have left you satisfied yet wanting more."
~ Fresh Fiction

Queen of Corvids
"It has all the classic comedy, angst, and drama that I have come to expect from J.C. McKenzie, and then it piles on mystery and more interesting characters."
~ Lady with a Quill

The Call of Corvids
"This is a fascinating read that brings together a world that has been marred with fae wars"
~ Fresh Fiction

Shift Happens
"SHIFT HAPPENS has excitement, intrigue and lots of danger. I love the whole cast of characters and how they played a part in the story"
~ Fresh Fiction

Beast Coast
"I loved this book as much as the first. There are secrets, surprises, and all manner of supernaturals."
~ Paranormal Romance Guild

Carpe Demon
"The story keeps the adrenaline pumping and spine tingling tension building throughout the story"
~ Literary Addicts Book Community

Shift Work
"If you like supernatural reads, with a side of romance, the sort with solid and intense plots, gripping and very real dangers, hard choices, supernatural people some of whom can be selfish, cruel and bloodthirsty...You'll be hooked."
~ Jeannie Zelos Book Reviews

Beast of All
"This time out, J. C. McKenzie has outdone herself with high-velocity action, soul deep emotions and one of those finishes that you want to replay over and over!"
~ Tome Tender

COPYRIGHT INFORMATION

This is a work of fiction. Names, characters, places, and incidents are either the product of the author's imagination or are used fictitiously, and any resemblance to actual persons living or dead, business establishments, events, or locales, is entirely coincidental.

Dark Legacy

COPYRIGHT © 2021 by J. C. McKenzie

Contact Information: jcmckenzie@jcmckenzie.ca

Cover Art: Eerilyfair Design

Publishing History:

First JCM Publications Edition, 2021

ISBN: 978-1-990143-07-6 (print)

ISBN: 978-1-990143-08-3 (ebook)

To my mother,
who not only encourages me to write,
but inspires me every day

Thank you

"I will not be another flower,
picked for my beauty
and left to die.
I will be wild,
difficult to find,
and impossible to forget."

— ERIN VAN VUREN

CHAPTER 1

"I take it you're not here for tea or to reminisce about our shared past."

— RAVEN, FLEXING HER
THINKING SKILLS

R aven sat on her throne of iron feathers and watched the arrogant Lord of War stomp down the aisle toward her and her guardian. Instead of wearing her customary court outfit, she'd opted for the leather armour favoured by the fae for stealth and increased mobility. Now, she regretted her choice. The leather chafed her neck and made her feel trapped in her own clothes. She wanted to shift into her conspiracy and leave before she had to tolerate a dark fae lord who most likely plotted her demise.

Instead, she remained seated in her human form and waited for the fireworks to start. What better time to question her life choices?

For six long, arduous years, Raven had worked tirelessly at this queen stuff. She fended off assassination attempts by disgruntled fae, ruled the Shadow Realm and controlled movement between the other domains. She had her *anam cara*, Cole, and her guardian, Rourke, by her side. Life had been good and relatively quiet.

Too quiet.

Because for six years, the Lord of War had bided his time, scheming for his golden moment of opportunity to take Raven down. What had Bane been up to all this time? Why seek an audience with her now? What had changed? What had her spies missed?

Bane pushed past the troll ambassador from King Tethaahin's court who stood near the bottom of the dais in front of Raven.

"Hey!" Iashindinn Kanwann protested. The ambassador turned to scowl at the fae who nearly bowled her over and hesitated. She bit off whatever she planned to say next and settled for glowering. Like all the descendants of Ymir, the ambassador had the characteristic gray skin and two ribbed horns protruding from her temples. Raven seldom encountered female trolls, but this one had long, lavender coloured hair pulled back in a low ponytail bound with a leather strap. Her thin lips peeled back to reveal jagged teeth, and a shiny triangular pendant around her neck glinted in the light.

Raven's birds perked up in delight. *Oooo shiny*.

The troll's honour guard standing along the wall shifted side to side, their gazes bouncing back and forth. They looked unsure of how to proceed.

No one knew how to proceed. The Lord of War had that effect on people.

Bane finally looked up the stairs to the dais where Raven sat on the throne and met her gaze. The Lord of War was back, all right. And he was certainly smug about it.

Raven hadn't heard what the troll ambassador wanted yet, and frankly, given Raven's history with the trolls, she didn't want to. Now faced with Bane, however, she might reconsider her stance.

Raven cursed. What a weak thought.

She was the Queen of Corvids, damn it. During her reign, many trials challenged her. She could face Bane. She could best him. For the love of Odin's balls, last time they'd met in conflict, she defeated him.

"Your eminence." Bane swept down in a shallow, mocking bow. He'd stopped at the bottom of the steps. Not so long ago she had faced the previous Queen from where he now stood. That meeting ended with the other woman's death. Would this meeting end with hers?

"I take it you're not here for tea or to reminisce about our shared past," she said.

"A tempting idea." His dry tone suggested otherwise.

She leaned forward on her throne. "What do you want?"

"What I've always wanted."

Rourke drew closer to the throne. He always protected her, watching her back in his black leather assassin's gear. As her blood-bound guardian, known as a *caomhnóir*, he had a vested interest in her continued existence, but he'd also grown to be one of her best friends. She trusted his judgement and opinions. He would die for her, literally, but she'd die for him as well. He was family, and that's what families did—torment each other mercilessly in one breath and in the next, fight for each other and help dispose of bodies in the dead of night.

"I want you to drop the barrier," Bane said.

Huh. That wasn't always what the Lord of War wanted. At one time, he'd tried to get her to erect a barrier. And she had.

Just not the one he wanted.

"I'm not dismantling the barrier between the realms," she said. Did Bane think she'd cower before him without Cole by her side? Her husband might be in an Underworld meeting with Odin, but she didn't need him to defend her or maintain her rule. "It's not exactly closed anyway. You're free to travel."

Bane narrowed his eyes and without speaking another word, she knew exactly what he thought and felt about her barrier. "I want unlimited, unrestricted, unmonitored travel to any destination of my choosing. I don't care what you do with the other Others."

Raven controlled the barrier that helped protect vulnerable regs—magicless humans occupying the Mortal Realm—from the powerful fae who'd otherwise prey on them in some way or another. Though Raven's barrier was artificially erected, a natural barrier had existed, long ago destroyed by the very humans she now sought to protect.

When the natural barrier collapsed from the actions of misguided scientists, hordes of vicious fae invaded the Mortal Realm. All accountings of the faepocalypse told stories of brutal and horrific events. Murder and mayhem abounded until Odin stepped in and laid down the law. Things settled for a few generations, but the majority of regs distrusted anything or anyone different, and a large number of fae itched to shrug off Odin's rules.

In a move to prevent Bane from inciting a second wave of slaughter in a bid for world domination, Raven flexed her own magic muscle and installed her version of a semi-permeable barrier.

And now Bane wanted her to take it down or give him a way around it.

She drummed her fingers on the armrest of the

throne and pretended to consider his request. "The answer is no."

"You might want to rethink that."

"You might want to rethink your attitude. I could just eliminate you now." Not that Raven was usually capable of killing someone unprovoked, but Bane tempted her to embrace a darker side.

Instead of appearing cowed, Bane's lips tugged up. "I thought you might resort to threats."

"I learned from the best."

Bane brushed at his court armour, though it shone and didn't look like it had seen dirt or blood in years. "Have you spoken to your family lately?"

Raven stiffened. "You came into my court to threaten my family?" She connected with the ether of the Shadow Realm and pulled her scythe to her. The weapon snapped into reality and she clasped the shaft as she stood. Dark fae energy swirled around her, saturating every cell in her body. Her scalp prickled and her already wavy hair coiled with the power thrumming through her veins. Even the warm summer air around her pulsed with energy. She might not kill unprovoked, but Bane has just poked the beast. She wouldn't tolerate threats to her family.

Bane smiled in the face of his impending death. Smiled and held up his hands. "Relax, Branwen Lulu Crawford. I wouldn't dream of harming my caomhnóir."

What?

She froze. The magic fell to her feet and faded away, leaving her drained. She wanted to sit down but couldn't in the face of this news. Bane had drawn out the pronunciation of caomhnóir, stressing the long "e" sound with a purr so it sounded more like keeeeeeeeeeeve-noyr instead of keevenoyr, but there was no mistaking the word, nor the implications. "What in the Underworld are you talking about?"

"Has no one told you? Your family has been extended to include a new member."

"Who?" Odin's shrivelled blue balls. The sense of dread twisted in her belly and tugged. She wanted to throw up. Instead, she swallowed and maintained eye contact. She knew the answer before it left his lips.

"Me."

"Impossible." No one in her family was stupid enough to let this snake into their den.

Bane examined his nails. "Oh, I don't know about that. I can be charming when I need to be."

"My family would never be charmed by you. They're more likely to gut you than welcome the Lord of War with open arms."

"Are you sure about that? The first part that is. I have no doubt of your accuracy with that last bit."

She snarled.

He bowed again, just as shallow, and just as mocking. "I see you haven't been informed of the changes to the family dynamic yet. I'll leave you now and call again at a later date. Maybe then you'll be more reasonable and we can have a more civilized conversation about how you will yield to me and grant my wishes."

He turned and walked away from the throne.

Raven squeezed the scythe. It wouldn't take much to reach out and extinguish him now when he least expected it. She was no longer the ignorant waitress from six years ago. With Cole and Rourke, she could defeat the Lord of War. But she hesitated. His words kept bouncing around in her head, caomhnóir and family. Had he bonded to someone in the Crawford family? Who? When? How? The guardian bond couldn't be forced. The connection had to be voluntarily and willingly offered.

If Bane spoke the truth, she couldn't smite him. Not when there was a chance it might kill someone in her family.

He took forever to saunter away, armoured boots hitting the black aisle runner with no sense of urgency. He even had the audacity to chat with some minor fae lord lingering near the exit. She forced herself to sit back down on her throne and wait. She mentally repeated all the reasons she couldn't kill Bane and squeezed her scythe to prevent herself from lashing out.

The troll ambassador approached the dais and bowed, but Raven ignored Iashindinn, not because she lacked manners, but to keep her attention focused on the Lord of War.

Bane looked up from his conversation and winked at Raven before turning to leave.

She waited until he exited the hall. "Rourke."

Her guardian stepped up to stand beside her, his feet barely whispering against the stone flooring. If he wished it, Rourke could be silent and had a near-perfect record from his days spent as a guild assassin. He'd only failed one job—killing an upstart half-fae raven shifter waitress.

Now he served her.

Willingly, of course.

"Yes?" Rourke asked.

"What is he talking about?"

"I have no idea." Rourke frowned so hard it looked as though his eyebrows were attacking his face. He flashed his pointed teeth at her. "I'll find out."

She shook her head. "We will find out together. Close the court. Cancel our audiences, grab Cole from the Underworld and meet me at my parents' place."

Rourke paled.

"We're going to the Mortal Realm."

"What about us?" The troll ambassador found her voice.

"Be glad I haven't killed you for stepping foot in my court," Raven replied. "I haven't forgotten what Nerthach and Gwawrddur did, and I don't owe you or your king a thing." Without a second thought, Raven sprung from her throne and pulled her magic around her.

CHAPTER 2

"We could always kill him after."

— ROURKE, HELPFUL AS EVER

Raven stepped from the shadow portal into her family's dining room, with Rourke and Cole trailing close behind. Rourke had taken mere minutes to locate Cole and extract him from the Underworld. Though Cole's own family was mired with pain and complex dynamics, he loved her family unconditionally and protected them with savage ruthlessness.

In order to gain enough strength six years ago to erect the barrier that now protected the Mortal Realm, Raven and Cole had bound their souls together, becoming each other's anam cara, and every day she got to wake up beside the man she loved. He had many names, many titles, but she called him husband. Most of the time.

Their bond allowed them to find each other anywhere and sometimes, especially when Cole experienced something intense, she *felt* the emotion and sometimes caught images through their soul connection. Right now, uncertainty vibrated through the bond, but no one besides her could tell just by looking at him.

Well over six feet, with broad shoulders and a commanding presence in his formal fae court armour, the Lord of Shadows looked ready to start a war. The black matte finish on the protective metal of his breastplate, gauntlets and tall boots muted the soft light from the room's chandelier and made her husband resemble a living shadow.

With features too chiselled to appear pretty, Cole was still devastating to look at. He always had a lethal, rugged edge to his expression, making him beautiful in the same way a tsunami about to crush a shoreline was beautiful.

He reached out and took her hand in his own and gave it a little squeeze.

Instead of chaos greeting Raven, Cole and Rourke, silence stifled the dining room in her parents' place. Mom, Dad, Mike and Lincoln sat at the table with untouched food in front of them, their expressions drawn and shoulders tight. No one was eating the bacon. All was not well in the Crawford residence.

She expected her twin brother Bear to be absent, but not her younger sister, Juni.

Where was Juni?

Mom's sullen expression and the deep bags under her eyes contrasted with the light pastels of her outfit. She favoured capri pants and blouses and as always, looked like a ginger-haired Stepford wife, but really, she was a nuclear bomb waiting to explode. Raven was now firmly in her thirties and the queen of a fae realm, but Elizabeth Crawford still held the power to intimidate her with *the look*.

Raven's stepfather, on the other hand, was the exact opposite of Mom. Terry had raised Raven and Bear as his own and despite his lean runner's body, he reminded her of a teddy bear. She'd give anything for one of his Odin-awful dad jokes right now to lighten the mood and help her pretend something terrible hadn't just happened.

Her youngest brother, Mike, sat still and glowered, the food heaped on his plate in front of him forgotten. Mike had an insatiable appetite. Only dire news would prevent him from eating.

The last person in the room was unexpected and had a complicated past with her family. Lincoln sat beside her baby brother and kept his gaze down, but his interlaced fingers did little to hide how much his hands shook.

"Where's Juni?" she asked no one in particular. Dread clamped her spine, filling in the unspoken words with Bane's and not liking any of her conclusions. She didn't bother asking about Bear. Out of her two missing siblings, her sister was the most likely candidate.

Mom pursed her lips. Dad flinched.

"She bound herself to Bane," Mike said. His matter-of-fact tone struck the silence like a death knell. They echoed in the room and kept repeating in Raven's head, long after Mike finished speaking.

Her brain had already reached that horrific conclusion. Bane had mentioned a caomhnóir and Juni was missing. It took only seconds for Raven to put two and two together, but Mike's confirmation acted like a sucker punch to the stomach all the same.

"Why in the Underworld would she do such an incredibly stupid thing?" Raven asked.

They turned to Lincoln in unison, who somehow managed to pale even more. He bowed his head and whispered, "She did it for me."

Without thinking, she gripped her magic and surged through the room. She blinked and she had Lincoln out of his seat and pinned against the wall. Holding him in place with one hand at his throat while the other held her scythe, she hesitated. Lincoln had grown from the pubescent boy she had thrown in the dungeons years ago. Now bigger than her, heavy with muscle, he'd trained with Rourke and

13

worked for her husband. Yet he hadn't attempted to defend himself. She held him by the throat with the steely grip of her hand and magic and he just...let her.

"I should've killed you six years ago," she hissed.

Lincoln swallowed, his Adam's apple moving against her palm.

"*Einin*," Cole placed his hand on her shoulder and squeezed. "Perhaps we should let him explain."

Lincoln's leather armour bore rips and slashes, the fabric stiff with what looked and smelled like dried blood. His face was cleaner, but maintained a red tinge, as if he'd splashed cold water over it or Mom sent him to the bathroom with a washcloth and told him to clean up the blood. He didn't have any wounds that she could see, which didn't fit with the tattered armour. Her family hadn't murdered him yet, so maybe there was more to this story.

"We can always kill him after," Rourke said.

"Fine." She opened her hand and released her magic. Lincoln's feet hit the ground, but he didn't run. He lifted his chin and waited.

"You were supposed to keep her safe," she said. That was his job. Raven's younger sister had already dealt with enough trauma, and Raven tried to shield her from the dangers the fae posed to her safety. Lincoln's sole purpose in her court was to protect and watch over Juni when Raven, Cole or Rourke couldn't. And up until this point, he'd been good at it. Excellent, even. He eliminated threats without Juni even knowing.

Though Lincoln had originally betrayed Juni six years ago, leading her sister to an abduction for a power-hungry hyena shifter gang, Raven had shown mercy, imprisoning the teenager instead of killing him. While in her dungeons, Rourke had chosen Lincoln as Juni's sparring partner. The two spent the last five and a half years beating each other up, but in a good, personal-growth kind of way. When Raven granted Lincoln his freedom at the beginning of the year, he'd chosen to stay and continue acting as Juni's sparring partner and protector. He'd proven himself loyal and dependable, and never gave her reason to regret her decision.

Until now.

Why would Lincoln betray them?

They'd come to trust him.

Like him.

Odin's shriveled nuggets. Raven had started to treat him like one of the family.

Did she make a mistake?

Had he used all this time to plot against them?

"I tried," he said, voice raspy. She'd almost crushed his throat in her initial wave of anger. "I was willing to die for her."

Raven frowned. Okay, maybe not killing him was a good thing. "Explain."

"Hikaru caught us in a transference spell—"

She held up a hand. "Who the fuck is Hikaru?"

Rourke stepped up to stand beside her, crowding Lincoln some more. "He's that kitsune I told you about."

"The one who tried to steal Juni's gift from Inari?"

Rourke nodded in unison with Lincoln.

A few weeks ago, the deity, also known as a kami, had summoned her sister to the Realm of Light. Instead of telling Raven or taking any of the dark fae assassins or sentinels willing to protect her, Juni let some random kitsune she'd just met escort her. In return, that man betrayed her.

Luckily, Lincoln arrived in time to protect Juni and had reported the incident to Raven. She hadn't had a chance to grill her little sister about it yet and it appeared as though she was missing a lot of the story. Lincoln had left some important elements out.

She turned back to Lincoln. "I thought you killed him."

"I did. Or at least I thought I did," Lincoln said. "He took a ninja star to the neck and had no pulse, but when I returned from taking Juni home, his body was missing. It took me a while to figure out why. Apparently, the only way to kill a kitsune is to cut off all their tails. In the meantime, Hikaru spent the time healing and planning an attack. He caught us in a spell, but I was the one who triggered it, so I was the one trapped inside a magical bubble with him."

Rourke frowned. "That makes no sense. Why didn't Juni use her beacon?"

Lincoln looked away. "I had it. Not that it would've done her much good, anyway. I was on Juni duty, remember? No one would've received her distress call."

Juni wore the amulet in a choker around her neck. Raven gave the receiving charm to Lincoln a few days ago, so this must've happened when she left court to visit the Underworld with Cole and Rourke. Though Lincoln was accurate about the outcome, it still didn't explain why Lincoln had Juni's amulet. "Why wasn't the choker on her neck?"

Lincoln cleared his throat, his cheeks growing pink. Interesting. "When the transfer spell activated, I instinctively reached out to grab Juni, but all I got was the choker when the spell ripped us apart."

"Wait a minute," Cole interrupted. "A transference spell is triggered by a person's essence and only transfers that person to the specified site. Hikaru might've gotten Juni's hair or something, but not yours. Why did you get caught in a trap laid for Juni? Why did you get transferred at all?"

"We were..." Lincoln looked away again, this time a full blush spread across his handsome face. "We were kissing."

Silence descended on the room again as everyone straightened and gawked. In order for Lincoln to trigger the transfer spell, he had to have part of Juni with him, or in him. Guess her tongue was enough.

Ew.

Rourke recovered first. "I thought she hated you?"

Raven shook the image of her sister's tongue in someone's mouth from her scarred mind and nodded. "She definitely hated you."

Lincoln shrugged, helplessly. As if he couldn't quite explain it himself. "I didn't hate her."

Rourke grunted, his way of acknowledging the truth. He knew them well, overseeing their training for over half a decade.

"So, let me get this straight," Dad piped up from somewhere behind them. "You stepped on the spell while my daughter's tongue was in your mouth and the spell transported both of you to an undisclosed location?"

Lincoln's gaze wildly searched the room, probably looking for an escape route.

"Yes, Dad," Mike said. "Way to keep up with us."

They all returned their attention to Lincoln, his cheeks now shades of pink and red. Raven studied the man in front of her. When she'd first met him, he was a scrawny teenager with boyish good looks. Though a reg, time at her court had hardened Lincoln into a deadly fighter. With his torn, blood coated, black leather packed with weapons, leather vambraces and dark pants tucked into armoured knee-high boots, he looked like a fae warrior who'd just returned from battle.

Her sister could do a lot worse.

"I would've died for her," Lincoln said. "I think I did die for her."

Raven stepped back to give him more space. Now that the anger had faded, her thoughts could flow freely. Lincoln wasn't the enemy here. Bane was. Raven needed to collect as much information as possible if they were to dig Juni out of this hot mess. "Tell us what happened."

He bobbed his head. "Juni was trapped on the other side of some sort of magical shield from me. I told her to leave. She used a lodestone, but I didn't recognize it at the time. I thought she used the hōju and was just happy she got away."

"The *what*?" Raven asked.

"The hōju. That was the gift Juni received from Inari. She made me promise to keep the nature of the gift to myself." He paused to look down at his hands. "I think she'll forgive me for breaking that promise now. The hōju can grant the holder an unselfish wish."

Okay, wow. Raven needed time to unpack that. Why hadn't Juni told her about the hōju? And why didn't Juni use the gift?

"I think she wanted to tell you about the hōju herself," Lincoln said.

She pushed all her unspoken questions to the side.

She'd get to all of them eventually. "So Juni used a lodestone and left you with Hikaru."

Lincoln nodded. "I only had my boot dagger, and he was well trained. I tried to do as much damage as possible." He hung his head. "But he was better than me. Stronger, faster, armed with a sword." He took a deep breath. "I don't remember much after I fell to the ground. When I woke up, Juni stood over me. I smelled flower blossoms, but I don't know why. Roses, I think. And something else. I don't even know why I would remember something like that."

Raven knew, but she kept quiet, waiting for the bombshell to drop.

"And Bane, the Lord of War stood behind her."

Well, at least that answered where the lodestone took Juni.

Cole cursed.

They all swore.

Raven knew it was coming, they all did, but Lincoln's news still sent a dagger of pain to her heart.

"What happened next?" She squeezed her eyes shut like it would somehow prevent the truth from becoming a reality.

"Bane told her to attend him. He called her his vixen guardian."

Rourke let out another string of curses, punched the wall and stalked off. His footsteps fell heavy against the stone flooring.

"No," Raven whispered. Juni must've bound

herself to Bane in return for him saving Lincoln. Surely, there had to have been another way.

"I told her I wasn't worth it," Lincoln rambled on. "She should've run and never returned. I would've gladly died knowing she was okay."

Raven nodded, feeling the truth of his words, the pain in his heart. "Did she say anything to you?"

Lincoln swallowed, his Adam's apple bobbing up and down again.

"What did she say?" Raven asked more forcibly.

"She said I was worth everything," Lincoln whispered.

The pain in his voice tore at her heart. Odin's balls. It would be so much easier to blame and kill him.

"You can't kill him, Einin," Cole said, his deep voice rumbling. Mostly silent since their arrival, he stood stoically by her side in his matte black armour. He didn't need to speak, she sensed his anger and his fear for her sister through their bond. Cole quietly seethed. He wanted to hurt Bane and the images she caught through their bond made her flinch. Apparently, Cole had quite the vicious imagination when it came to revenge. While she wanted Bane dead, Cole had already run through numerous painful ways to achieve the Lord of War's death.

"I know we can't kill Lincoln." She'd never take away the person her sister loved. Juni didn't form serious relationships. In the last six years, she'd hardly dated, trying to keep things casual and her dates at a distance.

At first, Raven thought her sister's detachment stemmed from her infatuation with Rourke. He'd helped save her from the hyenas when she was fifteen and an unhealthy obsession resulted.

Then Raven realized the truth. Juni had recovered from her Rourke crush. From all accounts, Juni still adored the weapon-warper, but he wasn't the reason she held back from relationships. Juni still struggled to emotionally heal from the abduction, Lincoln's betrayal and being used to hurt Raven. Her sister sacrificed her love life because she didn't want to make Raven vulnerable again.

Raven squeezed her eyes shut again. Juni would never have had to bear those scars if it weren't for her. If Raven hadn't become the Corvid Queen, Juni would never have been abducted in the first place and she certainly wouldn't have been in a position where she had to bond to Raven's sworn enemy to save Lincoln.

Juni's actions spoke more than words. She cared for Lincoln. A lot.

"I can't kill him," Raven repeated, more to herself.

"I wish you would," Lincoln said. "I deserve it."

She shook her head. "No, you don't. You did nothing wrong. Juni made a huge sacrifice for you, which could only mean one thing."

"What?"

Raven forced a smile onto her face. "Welcome to the family."

"Apparently we're letting anyone in, now," Mike grumbled, but his heart wasn't in it. How could it be? He probably racked his brain, just like her, thinking about Juni and how to correct this unfortunate turn of events. And if the genius in the room couldn't come up with a solution, they were all in trouble.

CHAPTER 3

"Welcome to the fae club."

— COLE CAMHANAICH

After deciding not to kill the love of her sister's life, Raven stepped back and studied her family more closely. Mom, Dad and Mike still sat around the dining table as if expecting to feast on the now cold bacon and pancakes instead of possible war with an Other Realm.

Wait a minute.

She squinted her eyes and studied their faces again —faces she could recall with perfect clarity on any given day. The family she'd do anything for.

Aside from her twin who was absent from this little

get together, and Juni who was left to some sort of personal hell at the hands of Bane, her whole heart was in this room. And despite the lines and bags formed from missed sleep and concern, two of them looked positively radiant.

"Why are you glowing?" she asked Mom and Mike.

Mom scowled almost as hard as Mike. "We don't know why. Something happened and we think it has something to do with Juni. I feel...different. I feel like...*more*."

"Some weird tingly shit woke me up and now my fox is fucking silver," Mike said. "Mom called it pretty."

"It is pretty," Mom turned to Raven. "Mine is silver as well and I have two tails."

"Two..." But only kitsune foxes had more than one tail and they hailed from the Realm of Light. "Oh no."

Mom nodded. "I think Juni somehow unlocked her divinity to save Lincoln and whatever she did affected all of us."

"But she couldn't use that hōju thing for something like that, could she? That would be a selfish wish, right?" Raven said. This didn't make any sense, unless she misinterpreted Lincoln's explanations. She'd planned to ask more about Inari's gift later.

"Bane," Lincoln's voice interrupted her scrambling thoughts. "Bane promised to unlock her divinity. She didn't know the price at the time, and I managed to talk her out of it."

"We know the bloody price now." Rourke returned to the dining room, his expression still solemn, his mouth tense.

"Bear?" Raven asked her Mom.

"Not returning phone calls," Mike said.

Mom quickly blinked and looked away, obviously, too upset to answer. Typical Bear. Being an asshat and hurting Mom's feelings. Ugh. She'd rip him a new one later.

She turned back to Lincoln. "You said you smelled blossoms when you regained consciousness?"

He nodded.

"You're also standing and as far as I can tell, not actively bleeding, so am I right to assume some or all of your wounds are healed?"

He nodded again.

Raven rummaged through her brain. "Inari must be involved somehow. Juni must've used the hōju for you, Lincoln, but I'm missing something. Why would Inari gift Juni with a wish? Why would she help? And why would you guys start glowing? We're only distantly related to Inari. Why would you have this much light divinity to unlock in the first place?" So many questions, her mind reeled with them.

Dad's frown in Mom's direction gave her away.

"Mom?"

Mom flinched and looked down at her hands.

"Mom! What haven't you told us?" Raven asked.

"I may have...I may have over exaggerated the distant part of our relationship with Inari."

"How much?"

"She's your great-grandmother."

Raven rocked back on her heels. No wonder Inari sent a light fae lord to spy on them. "And how'd the divinity get hidden? Bear and I struggled to hide our dark fae nature our whole lives."

"My mother did something when she was pregnant with me. She didn't go into details. She wasn't one to share personal information. Whatever she did, she caused the roller DNA and the associated magic to become locked inside of her. That's why we take after the shifter side of the family more—the roller genes have been magically suppressed this whole time."

Most people in the Mortal Realm referred to those from the Realm of Light as rollers. Though the Crawford siblings had known they possessed roller ancestry, none of them had shown any of the characteristic magic of most rollers. Aside from her and Bear, who took after their dark fae father, the rest of her family all presented like typical fox shifters. At least until now.

"Why didn't I feel anything when it got unlocked then?" Raven glanced at Cole.

Her husband shrugged. "You're mostly dark fae. Bonding to Rourke and myself should've released anything else hidden."

She opened her mouth.

"No, I don't know why your bonding didn't affect your whole family when Juni's did. It probably has something to do with your dark fae genetics. Maybe it keeps the light stuff locked up."

This was unchartered territory for all of them. "Or maybe we didn't inherit the supressed light fae genes."

He smiled, a slow sexy smile that should've been given in private because she knew without a doubt he was thinking about doing naughty, naughty things with her. "You know I love it when you talk science to me."

"Gross," Mike said.

Rourke grumbled in agreement.

She winked at her husband and turned back to Mom and her brother. "Aside from feeling *more*, the glowing and the colour changes of your fox forms, have either of you noticed any other changes?"

Mike grumbled and Mom blushed.

Raven leaned in. Mom never blushed. Elizabeth Crawford simply wasn't the type. Too straight forward and indomitable, she'd never let something like embarrassment get in the way of communication.

"Spill it," she said.

Dad cleared his throat. "An increased sex drive."

Ew. Raven might be in her thirties and married, but the last thing she wanted was a visual of her parents acting on that increased sex drive.

"Welcome to the fae club," Cole said, dryly. If he wrapped his arm around her right now, she'd have to smack him.

"Gross," Mike said, again.

"Agreed," Rourke said. "But not untrue. The increased sex drive in fae is well documented. It's often the reason highly intelligent fae will do incredibly stupid things." Her guardian glanced at her.

Traitor.

"It takes a while to get a handle on it. Young fae tend to be more volatile." Cole explained horny fae like he would a geology lesson—dead-panned.

"Any new powers?" Raven interrupted the stimulating conversation. "Aside from getting it on?"

"Not that I've noticed," Mike said.

"We could run some tests," Cole said. "There's a trial young fae complete to learn the extent of their powers. I had Raven go through the tasks unofficially when she first became the Queen of Corvids. We could arrange for something similar for you guys."

"But later," Raven said.

Everyone's expression returned to the grim ones they wore earlier. Yes, later. After they figured out a way to save Juni.

CHAPTER 4

"Is this going to be one of those conversations about feelings?"

— ROURKE, DEFINITELY NOT
WANTING TO TALK ABOUT HIS
FEELINGS

Raven paced in Juni's basement bedroom while Rourke and Cole waited. They may have seemed affable in the dining room with her family, but anger rippled through her bonds with both men. They weren't angry with her but the situation. Her sister's room might seem like an odd place for them to go for planning, but at one time, this room had been Raven's. Plus, the main floor had no privacy and the rooms upstairs no soundproofing.

"Rourke." She stopped pacing and turned to face her guardian. "Please tell me there's a way to undo the caomhnóir bond."

His grim look conveyed his answer.

"Besides death," she added. Obviously, that wasn't an option.

"Only the one who holds the bond can break it," Rourke said, confirming her fears.

"Crap."

"You could release me from my oath at any time, *mo bhanrigh*." Rourke used the fae term for "my queen," probably to soften the blow.

Double crap. Why couldn't there be an easy solution? Why couldn't she find some sort of magic wand, wave it around, and utter some fae words to release Juni from a life of servitude to a narcissist.

Wait. Rourke said she could release him at any time. Did he want her to? He'd volunteered for the role, but maybe things had changed. "Would you like me to release you?"

"Not at all. I like my job and from what I hear, the breaking of a guardian bond is not pleasant. Besides, I've found my time at the Corvid Court highly entertaining and rewarding."

She narrowed her eyes. He had such a nice way of saying he found her dumbass decisions amusing.

"Is the breaking of the bond painful for the holder of the bond or the guardian?"

"Both," he said.

"But survivable?"

Rourke nodded.

"Then that's what needs to happen."

"Bane will not voluntarily release his only bargaining chip and insurance policy," Cole said.

"We need to find something he values more," she said.

"There is good news," Rourke said. "He will not harm her. He will feel her pain and despite being the Lord of War, feelings of discomfort are not something he relishes. He only likes to inflict it on others."

"And he won't kill her," Cole added.

No, he wouldn't do that. He'd spent too much time and energy manipulating her sister into this. At least she assumed that's what happened.

"We could let time run its course." Rourke held his hand up to stop her protest. "I don't like it either, but can you see Bane tolerating Juni for an extended period of time?"

They all chuckled.

Juni was relatively safe and probably making Bane miserable. Was that what Juni was doing right now? Was she okay? Where was her sister? If only Juni were here to tell them what happened. Instead, they only had Bane's vague comments and Lincoln's half of the story.

"He'll push boundaries, though," she said. "He'll push and push and push, knowing we won't kill him. It's what he'll try to do while he has my sister as a shield that concerns me."

Both men scowled in agreement.

"We need to get Juni away from him," she said. "He probably has her at that portal-free cabin. We can't get to her unless she finds a way to draw blood and summon one of us."

"Even if she does, we're not going," Cole said, voice firm.

"Why not?" She wouldn't ignore a summons from any of her siblings.

"Besides being a possible trap?" Cole snarled. "No reason."

"I would've burned the Lower Mainland to the ground, consequences damned, to find Juni when the hyenas took her. Why do you think a possible trap would stop me now?" She called her magic and the scythe popped into existence. She held the shaft tightly and squeezed. This weapon was so much better than one of those stress balls. "We defeated Bane once and I only knew a fraction of what I do now. I don't fear him."

"You should," Cole growled. "He taunted you and kept Juni away. He wants you to follow."

"Then I'll fucking follow." She shook the scythe. "That cabin can fit six people in the largest space. If I bring you and Rourke, we'll have enough strength to take Juni with us. We just have to figure out a way to get there."

Someone cleared their throat by the basement door, and she whirled around to find Lincoln standing in the doorway, arms folded in front of his chest and leaning against the frame. He'd attempted to clean up even more and now wore a pair of her brother's jeans and an old T-shirt that fit too tightly across the chest and arms. His black hair still dripped from a recent shower and if Raven didn't know any better she'd think he was fae.

Rourke stood beside Lincoln and Cole appeared unsurprised, so only Raven had lost touch with her surroundings. She hadn't heard him approach at all.

Six years as the Queen of Corvids and she still had a lot of room for improvement.

"What?" she snapped.

"Juni has her choker," Lincoln said.

His words hit her brain like little slaps. Juni's choker acted as an emergency beacon, but it also acted as a sneaky little tether for portalling. No barrier could stop them from relocating to it.

"I thought you had the choker," Rourke said.

"I did, but then I threw it back to her before Bane hauled her off through a portal."

Raven let out a long breath and some of the tension clamping her shoulder muscles eased away. "Why hasn't she used it then?"

"Because it's a trap," Cole muttered.

Oh, her husband could get so testy when her life was potentially in danger. She'd yet to allow him to stuff her in a padded room, though, and she wouldn't start now.

"She's my sister, Cole," she said. "Don't expect me to sit back."

"I know better than that." He stomped away and opened a portal in the corner of the room. The shadows swirled around and caressed her shoulders.

"Where are you going?"

"To get reinforcements," Cole spoke over his shoulder. "If we're off on a rescue mission, I don't want to leave your family or our home vulnerable. That might be what Bane wants. Give me a few hours to mobilize a team into place."

Without another word, he stepped into the shadows with his cape swirling around him and disappeared.

Odin's balls, she loved that man so much.

"I want to come." Lincoln spoke with a firm voice, the kind someone used when they expected an argument.

She didn't have the energy to fight him, especially when she couldn't think of any reason to hold him back. She'd heard the agony in his voice and seen his pained expression, full of self-loathing and blame for not protecting her sister. He'd do anything to see Juni safe and that meant they finally had something in common.

She nodded and tossed a lodestone at him. "Get what you need and meet us back here in an hour."

Lincoln caught the lodestone but hesitated. "What are you going to do?"

She turned to Rourke. "Have a candid conversation with my caomhnóir."

The weapon-warper stiffened and glanced at the door. "Is this going to be one of those conversations about feelings?"

She nodded.

Rourke paled. "I'm not sure I'm going to like this."

He was so right about that.

CHAPTER 5

"Bane is only known for two things and they both begin with F."

— RAVEN, STATING THE OBVIOUS

R aven waited until Lincoln's footsteps disappeared up the stairs before she fully turned to her guardian. "Rourke."

"Branwen." He crossed his arms over his leather armour.

She narrowed her eyes at him. He knew how much she loathed her birth name. "I've never asked you anything personal."

"You ask me personal shit all the time." His

pointed teeth glinted under the artificial lighting. "I just refuse to answer."

"Asking you how your night off went or what your favourite drink is doesn't qualify as personal questions."

He scowled and unfolded his arms. "We're going to have to agree to disagree on that one."

She mimicked his scowl in hopes of getting a response.

He remained motionless and unresponsive.

"You have a past with Bane," she said. Maybe if she eased into the topic, he'd stop impersonating a gargoyle.

He stiffened and pressed his lips tightly together.

"May I ask the nature of that past?" she prompted.

"You may not."

She sighed. "This is for Juni, Rourke. I wouldn't ask otherwise."

He opened his mouth only to shut it again.

"Bane is only known for two things, and they both begin with F."

He raised his eyebrows.

"Fighting and...fornicating."

He snorted.

"I can't give him the fight he's after. The Mortal Realm would never survive a second faepocalypse. Do you know what he would want more than my sister as an insurance policy?"

Rourke paled, his gaze cutting to the only physical exit to the room.

Silence crept into Juni's bedroom like a deathly plague while her guardian battled with his internal thoughts. Raven waited, knowing full well he wouldn't flee. He'd tell her the truth. Not for her, not because of their bond, but for Juni.

Raven's biggest strength was also a weakness—her family. She made no secret of how much she loved her siblings and parents, and the whole Realm of Light and Underworld, including Bane, especially Bane, knew she'd do anything for them. Since no one in her family would let her ship them off to a secure location or wrap them in bubble wrap, they promised to accept Cole's shadow assassins as twenty-four-seven guards and work on decreasing their vulnerabilities.

Rourke had spent years preparing Juni for Bane's eventual attack. Almost six years of mentorship. He loved Raven's younger sister as if she were his own and without discussing any of those feelings Rourke tried to avoid, she knew Juni's current situation cut him deeply.

Rourke took a deep breath, his expression softening, his posture easing into something more relaxed.

"Me," he said.

"What?"

"Bane wants me," he said. "Or at least he did at one time."

Rourke's words hung heavy in the air and silenced

all the other thoughts rummaging around in Raven's head.

"Like...sexually?" she asked.

She'd never seen Rourke with anyone romantically. She just assumed he was asexual or kept his private life intensely private. She didn't really care what he did or who he did it with. The only thing that mattered to her was that he was happy.

A secret romance with Bane? Now that was a surprise.

"No, not sexually," he said.

"Oh."

"Not anymore."

"Oh." She really needed to read a thesaurus and improve her vocabulary.

"About a century ago, during the faepocalypse, I worked in his court. We became close. He demanded I become his guardian. Not his anam cara, but his guardian." Rourke's stern expression tightened. "He didn't trust or love me enough for the former, nor did he deem me worthy. He wanted a relationship where he had all the control. He might be known for fighting and fucking, but underneath it all, he's a control freak. When I said no, he lost it and I left. Bonding to you instead of him has only fed his anger. Bane covets what others have. What was once disposable becomes motivation for a new war." His face softened, almost in resignation. "There's always the possibility he might not want me now. Hurting you and me by bonding

Juni, might be just an added bonus to another devious plot, but that's a chance we will have to take."

Wait a hot second. He better not be suggesting... "You will not sacrifice yourself for Juni."

"Respectfully, that's not your decision to make."

She glowered at him. "Respectfully, you need me to release you first before you can run off and do something stupid."

He quirked his lips and shrugged. "Juni's worth it."

Raven hesitated. She'd always assumed Rourke loved Juni like a sister. As a fae, he had an extended lifespan that bordered on immortal and Juni had been an impetuous teenager with a crush when they first met. He certainly avoided her affections, and her numerous attempts to throw herself at him over the years. He never acted inappropriately. Had his feelings changed? Had he grown to love her in a different way now that she'd grown up? Did he hold back because she was still too young, because he was immortal, or because Lincoln, his protégé was clearly in love with Juni as well? Or all of the above?

Or did Raven read too much into this situation and his last comment?

"Of course, Juni is worth it, but so are you." Raven jabbed him in the chest with her forefinger.

Ouch.

Rourke's smile widened. "She's your sister."

"And you're family, too. Don't you even think about bonding yourself to that masochist. Trading one family member for another won't change our situation. We'll find another way."

Rourke's smile faltered. "Bonding to Bane would be most unpleasant."

She nodded. "He's a hot mess."

"In a designer suit," Rourke agreed.

CHAPTER 6

"I like stories where women save themselves."

— NEIL GAIMAN

R aven stood in her parents' basement with Cole, Rourke and Lincoln. Wearing full fae armour, the men were something to behold —beautiful and frightening all in one. Under different circumstances, she'd haul Cole to some private location and demonstrate her appreciation, but this was not the time or place. Right now, she noted their magnificence and mentally moved on. Her mind had one single focus —save Juni.

"I still say this is monumentally stupid and we're most likely walking into a trap," Cole said.

She pursed her lips and turned to him. "Do you have a better idea?"

"If I did, we'd be doing it," he muttered.

Typical. "Then let's do this."

Lincoln stepped in with the locator stone.

Cole reached out and clasped his shoulder. Rourke on the other side of Lincoln mirrored his actions. To complete the circle, Raven raised her arms and gripped her lover's shoulder with one hand and her guardian's with the other.

Their magic hummed with hers, vibrating stronger and stronger with the continued connection. Her power strengthened with theirs and if Bane made the mistake of crossing her now, she had enough magic to snap him in half.

And destroy her sister in the process.

The reality check sucked away her anger and settled like a lead pit in her stomach. She needed to stay calm when they confronted Bane. She could not afford to lash out.

Lincoln's eyes widened as their power flowed in a circuit through their bodies. As a reg, he had no access to fae power or supernatural abilities, but over the years, he'd developed a sensitivity for it.

The magic thrumming through her veins vibrated in the air and radiated out as if she were the centre of a bonfire. It was time.

She nodded at Lincoln.

He swallowed and concentrated on the locator.

Shadows rose and swirled around them, faster and faster. Wind whipped her hair around and ruffled Cole's long black cape.

The portal carried them through the Shadow Realm to the Realm of War, reforming the group in a small log cabin within the Underworld. Dark energy swirled around them, teasing and tempting.

The smell of wood and a burning fire filled her nose. Cute plaques decorated the walls and contrasted with the occupant's personality to the point of being creepy. Exactly who did Bane hope to fool?

She did not have fond memories of this place.

"Ah. Just like old times," Bane crooned from where he sprawled on the couch in jeans, combat boots and a long-sleeved Henley. He'd pushed the sleeves to his elbows and looked ready to hang out to watch the game, not incite an inter-realm war.

Juni sat across from the Lord of War with her arms folded over her chest. Dried blood crusted her clothing and sweat had matted her curly red hair into one giant frizzy knot. She wore a scowl, but otherwise appeared unharmed.

No one else was in the cabin.

Odd.

Tension released from Raven's shoulders, but she kept a firm grip on her scythe.

"Are you okay?" Raven asked Juni.

"I am the farthest thing from okay," Juni snapped.

Right. Okay. Baby sister was fine.

Instead of snapping back at Juni, Raven remained where she was and watched the Lord of War. If she attempted to grab Juni and whisk her away, would Bane try to prevent it? Did he have Juni booby-trapped? What was he up to?

Bane smirked as if he found the entire situation highly amusing.

Raven swallowed all the words she wanted to say. "Tell me what you want and release my sister."

Bane laughed, one of those loud, over-the-top, condescending laughs. "I already told you what I want."

Right. He wanted unrestricted, unmonitored passage through the Shadow Realm to reap havoc on the Mortal Realm. Raven never considered herself altruistic. Though she'd prefer to protect the Mortal Realm where her family and friends currently lived, she still considered it. She could move her loved ones to safety in time and her barrier hadn't been in place for that long. The Mortal Realm had survived without her protection for generations. Maybe they could again.

Maybe the unrest among the fae had cooled.

And maybe it would be a hot, hot mess.

Worth it. "If I drop the barrier, you'll release Juni?"

Lincoln grunted.

Juni's gaze flicked to him and her entire demeanor changed. The stiffness in her spine disappeared and her scowl softened.

Oh dear. Her sister had it bad.

Bane laughed again and this time, Raven used every ounce of self-control not to launch across the room to make him bleed.

"Why would I do that?" Bane asked, obviously not expecting an answer. "She's my only insurance policy, my only guarantee you'll do as I ask and not kill me at the first possibility."

"I'll swear a fae oath."

Cole growled.

She waved him off.

"Not good enough. You'd proven quite adept at working around the restrictions of an oath already."

Why would she grant him this request if he had no plans to release Juni? "I don't understand."

"Probably not the first time that's happened." Bane's smirk was back and just as insufferable. Maybe she could just hurt him a little. Not enough to kill him, but enough to make him regret crossing her family.

Cole snarled. "Why would Raven grant your wish if you're not willing to release Juni?"

Bane's smile widened. "So I don't make the queen's little sister's life miserable."

"You're making all our lives miserable," Raven said. "You didn't need my sister as your caomhnóir to accomplish that. Cut the crap. You won't harm her and we won't kill you, so we're at a stalemate as far as threats of torture, maiming and murder go."

"Could've just said bodily harm," Rourke muttered under his breath beside her.

Seriously? What had she done in a previous life to get such a smart-mouthed guardian?

"What are you offering?" Bane sighed and straightened in his seat. His arrogance was nauseating. He hadn't bothered to stand since their arrival. He was full of disrespect, confidence, or shit. Probably all three, but his casual posture didn't fool her or make her forget she stood in the presence of a talented warrior. She'd seen Bane and Cole clear a room of guards. Well, mostly. She caught the tail end of the massacre, anyway. She'd never underestimate the threat Bane represented, no matter how comfortable or relaxed he appeared.

"I'll give you what you want, but the price is releasing Juni."

"No deal."

"Then ask for something else, but just know, I won't trade for anything less."

A sly grin spread across the Lord of War's face and she couldn't stop the groan escaping her lips.

"I'm sure I'll think of something," he said.

She could think of a lot of things to do to Bane, but they all ended up with him dead or holding his guts in his hands. Raven didn't want to stay in this creepy cabin exchanging banter with the dark fae lord any longer than necessary. Her control over her own need to lash out had its limits. "You know how to reach me. In the meantime, Juni's coming with us."

Bane laughed and reached into his pocket. He pulled out a small gray lodestone and tossed it at her sister.

Juni caught the disc from the air. Recognition sparked in her gaze and she grimaced. Without taking her eyes off the Lord of War, Juni stood and crossed the room to join Raven. The second she came within reach Lincoln held his hand out.

When Juni took his hand, he pulled her closer. They didn't hug or kiss or whisper gushy stuff about their feelings, but they stood close enough for Juni to lean into him and breathe the same air.

Aww.

"You may have your sister." Bane stood in one swift motion, his arrogant voice ruining the sweet moment between Juni and Lincoln. Probably as he intended because he was a bastard like that.

The light from the roaring fire flickered across Bane's face and cast half his expression in shadows. "Juni could use some training in fae magic and manners while you're at it."

Raven and Juni turned in unison and flipped him off. Raven had never been more proud of her baby sister.

Ignoring Bane, Raven gathered the group and Cole took them away, dancing along the shadows of his power back to the Mortal Realm and safety. They'd retreat today, but tomorrow, they'd find a way out of this mess for Juni.

CHAPTER 7

"People say nothing is impossible, but I do nothing every day."

— A. A. MILNE

Cole opened the portal in the alley outside her parents' home, for which Raven was grateful. Last she saw Mom and Dad, they looked ready to either blow up or pass out. Portalling into their kitchen with their lost daughter might just give one of them a heart attack and no one wanted that. Besides, Raven needed some fresh air.

"Go inside," Raven said to Juni and Lincoln.

With grim faces, they held hands and walked to the

gate in the back fence. They didn't even try to talk back.

"I'll go with them," Cole volunteered.

She smiled at him. They all knew the firing squad, also known as Mr. and Mrs. Crawford, would ambush those two the moment they stepped inside. Mom had a soft spot for Cole and his presence would help smooth over Juni's return home.

"Thank you," she called out.

He paused at the gate to look over his shoulder and wink. "You'll owe me."

"Gladly." Her body hummed with anticipation. Her skin heated with the tease of a memory from the night before. Time had done little to lessen the need that consumed her anytime Cole was near.

Rourke frowned. "When are the two of you going to get sick of each other?"

"Hopefully never. If he remains infatuated with me, he'll never see my flaws."

Rourke shook his head. "They're hard to miss."

"Hey!" She punched him in the arm.

He didn't try to dodge or block, which said exactly how little she scared him.

The wind whispered down the alley, and she lifted her face to catch the breeze.

"We both know he sees all the flaws. He loves you for them, not despite them." Rourke crossed his arms over his chest. "It's quite sickening, really."

"He might love my flaws, but he'd also love to lock me away from harm."

"Also, very true. I'm glad he hasn't succeeded with that. It would make my job incredibly boring. If he ever does manage to lock you up, don't worry. I'll break you out." Rourke leaned in. "We have company."

"I know." Raven turned to face Iashindinn, the troll ambassador with lavender hair, and her small contingent of guards. "Showing up at my parents' place in the Mortal Realm is an act of war."

The troll flung herself on the ground. The loose dirt crunched under the impact. "My deepest apologies, *bhanrigh*. You cancelled my audience and ignored my last attempt to speak with you."

Raven scowled. On Earth, they called that a hint.

"I know our people have given you no reason to do us any favours, but we need your help."

Well, wasn't the ambassador painting the past in pretty pastels? Six years ago, two prominent members of troll society, Nerthach and Gwawrddur, had attacked Raven after Juni had gone missing. If the trolls had managed to hurt or kill Raven, Juni's fate would've been drastically different.

"I owe you nothing," she hissed. "Not even my time."

Rourke placed his hand on her shoulder. "I think they want to owe you."

She narrowed her eyes at the troll flattened against the ground. The whole thing felt wrong—both the troll cowering before her and Raven's lack of empathy. Six years was a long time to hold a grudge. She'd released Frey, a fae with a smidge of corvid essence, a number of times from her dungeons, giving him chance after chance not to be an asshole, and he kept coming back trying to kill her for her crown.

So what was the difference?

Frey and the trolls had both tried to harm her, but Frey's actions only affected her. While Raven could handle threats to her own life, she was unwilling to accept the possible harm to her family.

That was the difference. Team Crawford for life.

But maybe she could ease up a little. The troll attack had been six years ago, after all, and they'd been unaware of her sister's circumstances. They hadn't intentionally delayed Raven to help the hyenas, nor were they responsible for Juni's abduction.

Raven released her anger and sighed. "What do you want?"

"Tuguh has been taken."

Raven lowered her scythe. The name sounded familiar. She rummaged around in her memories of Cole's training sessions. "The troll king's only son and heir?"

The troll nodded against the pavement.

"You may stand."

The troll scrambled to her feet and brushed off her clothes. "All our attempts to locate him have failed."

"Why come to me?" Raven assumed she'd be the

last person on the trolls' friend list. The grudge worked both ways last time she checked. Though Raven had asshole-like tendencies from years of working in the service industry, she had reached out to the troll monarch once she'd settled into her role. Also known as jotun, the trolls held a powerful position in the realms, namely controlling troll toll bridges in the Mortal Realm and handling large inter-realm currency exchanges. They would make better allies than enemies.

She'd naively hoped Nerthach and Gwawrddur had acted independently, but King Tethaahin had disavowed that notion. His treatment of Raven and blatant lack of respect made it clear what his thoughts were about the new Queen of Corvids. Since then, Raven mostly ignored the trolls and tried to forget they existed.

Iashindinn was making that very difficult at the moment.

The troll stared at her feet. Her stone-coloured lips pressed together. How many other people had they gone to for help?

"You've already tried everyone else you think would be helpful?" Raven guessed.

The troll shook her head. "To admit weakness to our enemies would carry catastrophic results."

"Am I not an enemy, Iashindinn?" Did her king even know his ambassador was here?

"Please, call me Iashi." The troll sighed. Her thin

lips revealed uneven teeth and black gums when she spoke, and she kept her unnerving black-eyed gaze focused on Raven. The light from the overhead streetlamps reflected off her lavender hair and made it look like glowing strands of silk.

Iashi wore leather armour better suited for her twisted figure than the metal plated armour the fae favoured. The leather creaked as she shifted her stance and visibly considered her next words before speaking. "We do not have an amicable past, that is true, but we've watched you from the infancy of your reign and you are not malicious. You do not move to capitalize on another's vulnerabilities just because you can. You seem content with maintaining your court and you're utterly ruthless at defending your own. We erred in moving against you."

Was that an apology? Or just flattery to butter her up?

"Besides, you slaughtered one of our best troll retinues, so technically, we've already shown you a weakness."

That actually made sense.

"Tuguh is an infant in troll years. He's innocent. Please do not judge him for his people's actions."

Raven frowned. She'd already decided to help them. "I still don't understand why you think I can help you when your own attempts have failed."

The troll bobbed her head as if she expected this question. "You can monitor the movement of all travel through the Shadow Realms, and you previously worked as a private investigator."

Yes, but there had to be more.

"And we knew if we mentioned a missing child, you'd help."

Ah, there it was. Her weakness. Her need to protect. Such a nice way to say the mighty Queen of Corvids was a soft touch. They weren't wrong.

"What information do you have? What did you find out during your own investigation?"

"Tuguh was taken from the castle four weeks ago. Your sentinels wouldn't disclose any information to us, but our own guards did not report any suspicious travel through the approved three-Ps. There's been no sightings, no ransom demands." She stopped talking and waited.

"That's it?"

She nodded.

"That's all you've got?"

"Yes," she hissed, apparently not too pleased with this fact herself.

"Who's in charge of the investigation?"

"I am...now."

Raven didn't miss the pause or its meaning. "Now?"

"The previous investigator is no longer in charge."

Oh dear. "I'll check with my sentinels, but they would've stopped anyone transporting a minor in distress or unconscious. If they were unable to apprehend suspicious travellers, they would've reported it and if they were killed in attempting to stop the travellers, I'd certainly hear about it. So either they smuggled him through or they found another way."

"There is no other way." Iashi glanced away.

Ah. Did the ambassador wish to keep the truth from Raven? Did the troll hope Cole had skipped that part of his very thorough lessons? "Correct me if I'm wrong, but don't the trolls have their own method of transportation to other realms?"

Iashi gaped at her. "But...But that..." she sputtered, obviously not happy that Raven knew about the troll tunnels or where her line of questioning took the discussion.

"That means an inside job," Raven said. "A troll or trolls betraying their own."

"Not possible."

"No?" The trolls she'd dealt with in the past were shady as fuck and tried to screw her over, but she wasn't a troll. Maybe they treated their own better. Maybe they had a sense of loyalty and due to Raven's own attempts to avoid the troll kingdom, she failed to see it.

"Not possible," Iashi repeated.

"We'll pursue all possibilities. Can you promise me and my party safe passage and that the trolls aren't working with or for Bane?"

She nodded.

"I need a jotun promise."

Iashi straightened and something flashed in her dark gaze. "You have my promise that you and your party will have safe passage to investigate the disappearance of Prince Tuguh and also my word that to the best of my knowledge no troll is conspiring with the Lord of War against you."

The power of the troll's promise eased some of the tension around Raven's neck and shoulders. "Will you take me through the troll tunnels if the trail leads that way?"

The ambassador shifted her weight from foot to foot and looked at her guards. Iashi's companions had stayed stone still and mute the entire time and remained that way when Iashi turned to them. She'd find no answers there. The ambassador sighed again, the weird hissing sound not as grating as when Raven first heard it. "Just you."

Raven shook her head. "I must insist on bringing either my caomhnóir or anam cara. I also need to bring one of my siblings."

"Why?"

"Protection."

She waved her hand as if to dismiss her answer. "Why your sibling?"

Raven tapped her nose. "We're going to track your baby troll the good old-fashioned way."

That didn't seem to reassure the troll at all.

CHAPTER 8

"I've got ninety-nine problems, but eighty-six of them are completely made-up scenarios in my head that I'm stressing about for absolutely no logical reason."

— UNKNOWN, BUT ALSO RAVEN

Raven paced back and forth and tried to form words. When she failed, she paced a little faster.

Juni perched on the end of her bed beside Lincoln, their hands clasped together, their thighs touching. They didn't look at each other though, they were too smart to take their eyes off Raven who now stood in front of them.

Raven studied her sister and her...whatever Lincoln was. She flicked her finger between the two of them. "When did this happen?"

Lincoln hadn't been forthcoming with details, and since they had other, more pressing concerns, like getting Juni extracted from Bane's evil clutches, she hadn't pressed.

"It's new." Juni straightened and lifted her chin. "Don't ruin it."

Raven rocked back on her heels. What in the Underworld? "Why would I do that?"

"Well, I don't know. But you've been pacing in front of us for the last ten minutes and you're starting to freak me out. Now you're facing off with us like you're about to scold us for being naughty children. I already have parents, thank you very much."

Raven snorted. Mom and Dad had grilled Juni about the events leading up to today and admonished Juni for her rash decisions. That wasn't the worst part, though. Now that it was clear to anyone with two eyeballs, that Juni was serious about Lincoln, Mom would want to talk to Juni privately about all the stuff. Raven didn't envy her sister. That was one awkward conversation.

Maybe Raven could hide in the shadows and listen in. They'd all survived the basic sex talk Mom gave when they were teenagers, but the impending discussions Juni faced would eclipse the previous ones. Raven knew from experience.

"I'm not going to scold you," she said. "I want to know what the fuck is going on."

Juni swallowed.

"I know Inari is our great-grandmother. You left that part out about your trip to the Realm of Light, by the way." When Juni went to Inari's court and took a kitsune she'd just met as her escort instead of telling any of them, Raven had to find out about it from the sentinels and Lincoln.

Initially, Raven had been angry. Pissed. Ready to tear Juni a new one, but Cole had placed his hand on her shoulder and asked her to think of what would happen if Juni had said something in advance. Raven would've gone. Or Cole. Or Rourke. And when Raven walked through all the possible outcomes of a summons from Inari, many involving traps or war with the rollers, Juni's motives became abundantly clear. Her baby sister didn't act irrationally or stupidly, she acted to keep Raven safe.

It was still reckless and stupid, but how could Raven get angry at her sister for something like that?

When Raven asked Juni about it, her sister had explained away the summons as Inari wanting to meet her because their neighbour Chad mentioned running into her. And now, thanks to Lincoln, Raven also knew Juni had left out a crap-ton of other information. Like Inari giving her a wish-granting hōju. The same gift the kitsune tried to steal from Juni.

"I didn't have the opportunity to speak with you

privately. I figured I had time to tell you later," Juni said.

"Like a text message wouldn't work?" Raven muttered.

"Mike's not the only one who can hack into messages. I try to avoid sending life altering information via text as much as possible. I wanted to keep the information about the hōju private. Not from the family, but everyone else. I'd just had someone try to kill me for it and I didn't know what people would do if they found out I possessed a hōju or discovered Inari was our great-grandmother."

Raven paused. That actually made sense, damn it. The knowledge of their relationship to Inari could and would be used against them and a wish-granting orb would tempt anyone with questionable morals. Juni was wise to exercise caution. If there had been an urgency to convey the information, Juni would've found a way.

"Lincoln filled us in with what happened up until he lost consciousness." Raven crossed her arms over her metal breastplate. "Somehow from then to the time he woke, you bound your life to Bane's and managed to heal Lincoln's wounds. We have theories, but I'd like to hear your story."

"You've been busy." Her sister sounded genuinely surprised Raven had dug for information. Honestly, Juni should know better than that.

"You seem to have forgotten how much you mean to me," Raven said.

"When you act like this, it's easy to forget."

Raven narrowed her eyes at her sister. Seriously? How did she not seem concerned with her sister's situation? "I think you made some sort of deal with Bane to free Lincoln and used the hōju to heal him. How am I doing?"

"Seems like you have it all figured out already," Juni grumbled.

Lincoln snapped his head to the side to gape at Juni. "So it's true? You used the hōju on me?" He didn't sound like he believed it.

She shrugged as if it were no big deal, but it was. In Juni's world, she may as well shout her love for this boy from the rooftop.

"Juni." Lincoln's grip on her sister's hand visibly tightened.

She lifted her chin. "Neither Bane nor I have healing abilities. I had already tied my life to that monster to break the barrier, release my divinity and defeat Hikaru. Seemed rather silly to let you bleed out at that point."

"You shouldn't have done it. You shouldn't have done any of this. I'm not worth it," Lincoln said.

Raven eyed the door. She still wanted to talk to her sister, but this conversation had quickly turned to make her feel like the awkward third wheel.

Juni pressed her lips together hard enough the skin around them turned white.

Oh dear.

"You two can bicker about this later," Raven said. "I need to know the specifics of the deal and if Inari said anything, anything significant."

"Which deal? The one with Bane or the one with Inari."

Raven pinched the bridge of her nose. "Both?"

"I swore my life to Bane's as his caomhnóir," she whispered, not looking away from Lincoln. "Pretty straight forward."

Lincoln flinched at the words but tightened his hold on Juni's hand.

Raven mentally cursed. No loopholes in that oath. "And Inari?"

Juni tore her gaze from Lincoln's and turned to her. "The deal with Inari was just as straight forward. I believe my exact words were, 'Please save Lincoln's life.' And aside from chastising me for my rash decision making, Inari didn't say anything."

Hmm. If their great-grandmother could grant Juni a wish for her sheer awesomeness, maybe she could grant another. Did the kami of grains, harvest, and agriculture have the power to break bonds between guardians?

Raven would have to ask. She didn't need a magic eight ball to know a visit to the Realm of Light was in her imminent future.

CHAPTER 9

"I'm already cursed with you as my brother."

— RAVEN TO MIKE

Mike stopped Raven before she left the house. She took a deep breath and braced for whatever he planned to say. Normally, her computer-loving brother had some sort of parting shot for her, usually one that insulted her intelligence or life choices. It was how Mike said, "I love you."

No insults today. Instead, her younger brother had a mean furrow to his brow and pursed lips. He had the same look when he got stuck trying to get through someone's firewall and anti-hacker defenses...or whatever that crap was called these days. She didn't see this look often, nor did it last for long. Nothing could deter her brother. Mike always found a way to get what he wanted or needed.

Technology and code spoke to him in the same way a good romance novel spoke to her. In elementary school, he constantly got in trouble for not applying himself or for talking back. It wasn't until a doctor conducted a psychological evaluation, that they discovered he was a bona fide genius, and that a lot of his behaviour and acting out was the result of boredom.

"What's up?" she asked.

"I need your help with a case."

She raised her eyebrows. "A case? Right now?" And he questioned her life choices.

He scowled as if he heard her internal thoughts. "I took the job right before Juni went missing. I planned to tell her about it, but she never returned from closing a cheating spouse case. At first, I assumed she finally hooked up with Lincoln."

"Well..."

He held his hand up to stop her. "Let's not go there. Anyway, I had counted on Juni's help with this case, but I don't think it's wise for her to leave the house without guards."

"Agreed."

"But I need to get this closed so we can all focus on Juni."

"You could drop it." Raven cringed the moment

she said the words. That's not how the Crawfords rolled. They always followed through with cases and they always delivered one way or another. Their closing rate and reliability was a point of pride for them all.

Mike's face twisted as if her words physically took a corkscrew to it. Admittedly, she had just suggested he tell the client he wouldn't work a case.

"I can't believe you just said that," Mike said.

"I'm stressed."

Mike grunted, his non-verbal cue for agreement. "Besides, we can't let the business go to shit. Juni will need a job to come back to and will never forgive us if we screw it up."

"You know you don't have to work, right? I have enough for—"

Mike levelled her with a Mom-worthy glare.

Right. What was she thinking? The entire family was stuffed full of stubbornly independent people, raised on the juice of being self-reliant and not taking handouts. They wouldn't let her shove them into protective care and barely tolerated the shadow assassin guards. They certainly wouldn't take her money. She'd set up accounts for them, of course, but they barely touched the funds she'd gifted them years ago.

Gah.

This infuriating feeling must be what Cole had to endure all the time. A tiny moment of sympathy washed over her, but in a blink of an eye, the feeling disappeared.

"Are you feeling okay?" Mike asked. "You're acting weird."

She frowned.

"Even for you."

"I'm not above smacking you," she reminded him.

"I'm divine now. You can't go around smacking gods. You'll end up cursed." He puffed his chest out. He'd been working out again.

She punched him in the arm, her fist smacking against hard muscle. He didn't try to block her and just grumbled from the impact.

"I'm already cursed with you as my brother," she said. "Now tell me about the case."

"There's a boy missing." Mike's words stopped all the snarky comments Raven planned to say.

"Dude," she said. "Why didn't you lead with that?" Even the trolls knew she was a soft touch when children were involved.

"Dude, you're way too old to use that word."

She narrowed her eyes at her brother. "Do you seriously want to argue with me right now?"

"No." His snarky tone contradicted his answer.

"Is this the Kayden Smith case?" It had been on the news non-stop last time she visited the Mortal Realm. The father's pleas for help and information had stabbed at her heart and filled her eyes with unshed tears.

Mike rocked back on his heels and shoved his hands in his pockets. "Good guess."

"Did the police contact you?" Sometimes the local PD contracted the family's PI business for cases that went cold.

Mike shook his head. "The father. What do you know about the case?"

"Not much. Last time I visited Mom and Dad, they had an amber alert out for him. That was maybe two weeks ago? Maybe a little longer?" Usually, she managed to sneak away from the Corvid Court at least once a week, but things had been busy lately.

Mike nodded and pointed at the stairs. She followed him to his room. Twenty-five years old and still living at home. She couldn't make fun of him, though—house prices and rent continued to sky-rocket in the Lower Mainland. Besides, she'd had to move back home in her late twenties. She couldn't judge even if she wanted to.

If anything, Mike staying home made her sad.

Mike could be making millions on his own. Instead of getting a corporate position, or selling his mad skills, he'd taken over the family private investigation business with Juni. He said it was all he'd ever wanted to do, but there was more to Mike's choices than family loyalty. He suffered from PTSD. If he didn't want to talk about his nightmares, though, she wouldn't push the issue.

Mike waved at the spare seat in his room, and she plunked down in the cushioned chair.

"Just over three weeks ago, eight-year-old Kayden Smith went missing from his family home. The father left him without supervision inside the locked house for an hour while he went to get groceries. When he returned, he found the home empty, door closed, but unlocked. With no signs of forced entry. No personal security system.

"Within twenty-four hours, three verified sources came forward claiming to see Kayden voluntarily get in a burgundy SUV with a female, Caucasian driver. Each provided a different model and make of the vehicle, but they all estimated the woman's age to be mid-thirties. She wore sunglasses. No one thought to record the license plate and none of the neighboring houses' home security cameras picked up the vehicle details either.

"The father had sole custody, so authorities zeroed in on the mother. She had an alibi and drives a white hatchback."

"Child services involved?" Raven asked.

"They were a part of the original investigation," Mike said. "Kayden was underage and shouldn't have been left unattended. The father may get charged with child endangerment. I think they're waiting to see the outcome of the missing persons case."

"And now there are no leads," she guessed.

Mike nodded. "The father contacted me two days ago."

"What changed? The police normally keep working child cases longer than this." Usually, parents of missing children didn't seek PIs until the police admitted the case went cold.

"Felicia Johnson."

"Who's that?"

"Kayden Smith's mom," Mike said. "She went missing."

Raven leaned back in the chair.

Mike continued to pace. "Police are still on the case. They brought in the alibi, but he's not talking."

"He'll talk to me." She could be very intimidating when she needed to be.

Mike stopped and turned to her, running his hand through his thick red hair. "No. He's literally not talking. He's been spelled. Can't speak or write. They're trying to find a witch to break it."

"Maybe we can sneak Marcus in." Her twin's bestie was a talented witch who also kept them supplied with charms and wards.

"Already tried. The lead detective doesn't want the possible witness contaminated by any magic users or shifters not vetted by the department." Mike scowled as he spoke.

"Sounds like a winner."

"Yeah." Mike frowned. "I don't actually think this one is anti-shifter, but he's worked in the system long enough to know his feelings won't matter. He's right to block us."

Unfortunately, regs had an ingrained distrust of shifters and witches, even though neither group had anything to do with the faepocalypse, the subsequent massacre, or the subjugation of regs by the fae.

"Does the alibi have a burgundy SUV?" Raven asked.

"No, but I like how you think. Like me. I went digging. The alibi has a sister." Mike paused dramatically.

She waved her hand in a circle for him to keep going. "And she has the SUV?"

"No. Keep up."

"I am keeping up. You keep pausing for theatrical effect and it's wasted on me."

"I need to breathe, you know."

"Even a god has limits? I'm shocked," she said.

He smirked and didn't speak for a moment. "She doesn't have an SUV, but she does have a cabin."

Raven sat up in her chair. Now, that was interesting.

"And three days ago, her keys went missing from her junk drawer."

"What an odd thing to notice," Raven said.

"What do you mean?"

"Do you check the contents of your junk drawer on a regular basis to take inventory?"

Mike rolled his eyes so well, Juni would've been proud had she been with them to witness it. "No, but if my brother was potentially involved in a missing child case, I'd check the junk drawer for my cabin keys to see if he'd taken them. Which is what the sister did, by the way."

"So what you meant to say is she *discovered* her keys were missing three days ago."

"Why are you...you?"

"What? Fabulous?"

"Annoying."

"Now you know how I feel." Raven smirked. Mike corrected her statements all the time, but she rarely had opportunities like this to return the favour. "Anyway, did the sister tell the authorities?"

"No. She didn't want to get her brother in trouble," Mike said, resuming his pacing. "I told them."

"And?"

"And they've found nothing so far."

She sagged into the cushions. Why would he build up the case briefing like that? "Did they take dogs with them?"

He shook his head. "They said there was no evidence to suggest the woman and son were present at the location."

"But you disagree?"

"I don't know enough to form an opinion, but it's our only lead and I'd like to check it out once they've officially released the scene."

Now his request for assistance made sense. "You'd like me to come."

"A nose on the ground..." he began.

"And eyes in the sky." She smiled, finishing his sentence. Working a case with her brother would be fun, almost like old times. Some of the tension knotting her muscles eased, but a sense of dread still hung over her shoulders. She'd do anything she could to reunite this missing boy with his father. She only hoped she'd find a way to save her sister as well.

And she also had her own side quest to complete now, thanks to the trolls.

"Speaking of helping out," she said.

Mike groaned.

CHAPTER 10

"I always wanted to be somebody, but now I realize I should have been more specific."

— LILY TOMLIN

In exchange for agreeing to work the case with her brother, Mike promised to go to Inari's court with Raven. As much as she wanted to shield him from every possible danger, going to Inari with Cole or Rourke would make the visit less casual. She didn't want to meet her great-grandmother under those conditions, especially when she planned to ask for help.

The police still hadn't released the mysterious cabin from Mike's missing child case, and as much as

Raven enjoyed sneaking around police officers stationed to guard the site, they opted to wait and avoid that particular complication. A high-profile case like Kayden Smith's meant at least attempting to do things by the book.

Iashi had also asked for a day to "set things up" in troll land. Whatever that meant. It didn't sound too inviting, but maybe the troll ambassador needed to remove all the fae-hating jotun from the crime scene to make the search for the missing prince safer for Raven and her team. Either way, Raven couldn't do much for the two missing children at the moment, but she could put some feelers out and hopefully set things in motion to save her baby sister from a lifetime of servitude with Bane.

Mike stood beside her, fidgeting with his outfit. Once a skinny computer geek, he'd grown into a strong, handsome man—the kind used for stock images of hot nerds. His red hair had darkened, bringing out the gold in his hazel eyes. He still had all his attitude and often shunned the spotlight and the attention he received when he went in public.

One day, though. One day, Mike would find someone, and he'd fall hard. She couldn't wait for that day. She had years of angst from all his sharp comments to retaliate with. The whole family waited, but aside from some casual dating, Mike seemed to have no urgency in finding someone special. He wasn't the dating douchebag like Bear used to be in his single days, Mike was just aloof. Distant. Completely opposite of how he was with the family.

"Stop playing with that." She hissed. Calling her scythe, the weapon materialized in her hand. In armored leather pants and a matching top, Raven wore a more subdued outfit instead of the battle bikini she was known for. Though she often complained about her revealing court attire, it certainly had its perks. One of which was keeping her cool. Full body armour was *warm*. And heavy.

Mike snarled but didn't argue, straightening beside her instead. "I still don't see why I had to wear one of Cole's sets of armour. I'm not a fae warrior. I fight my battles with a keyboard, and this makes me feel like an imposter. It's like playing dress up and it's very, very wrong."

"At least you look good in it." And he did. He looked like a bona fide destroyer of hearts and so very much like her twin. She had to bite her tongue to stop from calling him Gingerbear. The last time she slipped, he froze her Canadian bank account.

Mike perked up at her compliment, his sour expression softening a little. "I do?"

She rolled her eyes and reached out to tighten one of his vambraces. "I told you. Fae are all about appearances. I can't bring Cole or Rourke without my actions coming across as threatening and they're not available even if I could. Cole's off mobilizing more of his army of assassins as if another faepocalypse will descend upon us at any moment and Rourke needs to watch Juni."

While Rourke doubted the Lord of War's feelings, having him guard Juni seemed like the best possible deterrent. None of them could kill Bane, not when his death would mean Juni's, but the Lord of War was also less likely to kill Rourke to get to his guardian.

At least that was Rourke's logic when he volunteered for Juni duty.

"I think Lincoln's already watching Juni," Mike muttered.

"It's so weird."

"Right? She's never liked anyone." Mike grimaced. "Except Rourke."

"Also, weird." Raven nodded. "But remember, before Rourke it was Lincoln. She gave up a lot to keep him breathing. Whatever it is between them, it's real and it's strong. And it's certainly not up to us to choose her person."

"It's up to us to destroy anyone who harms her." Mike nodded, more to himself.

"Exactly. Now straighten up and hold my hand."

Mike scowled again and slapped his large hand in hers. She closed her eyes and called her power. The energy of corvids rose along with the power of the Shadow Realm. The magic curled around her, caressing bands of vibrating energy, and carried her off with her brother to the Gathering Place.

As the Queen of Corvids, she could use her power

to punch through her own barrier and travel directly to Inari's court, but she didn't want to incite a war. In addition to magical training, weapons training and combat defense training, Cole had spent a large portion of time explaining the intricacies of the realms and how fae politics worked. He really shouldn't have needed all that time. He could've just said she'd start a war if she broke any of the rulers' weird rules and that would've covered about ninety-five percent of the content.

The Gathering Place crystalized around her and Mike pulled his hand from hers as soon as the ground solidified under his feet.

Like a floating Stonehenge with portals instead of giant rocks, they stood in the centre of a round chunk of rock. An endless blue sky surrounded the Gathering Place with nothing visible in the distance, above or below the platform.

Illusion at its best.

Dark shadows solidified from behind each portal. Large dark fae warriors stepped from the shadows to stand between each of the swirling entrances to the courts within the Realm of Light. The warriors' matte armour absorbed the sunlight instead of reflecting it and their capes swirled around them identifying them as agents of her court.

Mike stiffened beside her.

Without a word, the warriors knelt and bowed their heads. Like typical dark fae, they were all gorgeous. Dark fae originated from the Underworld before the collapse of the original magical barrier. They had a wide range of physical traits from height, hair colour, skin tone and build, but the two common-alities were jaw-dropping attractiveness and black irises that bled out to cover the whites of their eyes when they experienced intense emotion or accessed their power.

Eyes of the Underworld, like hers.

"You may rise," she said.

Her brother relaxed.

A vaguely familiar dark fae rose and approached. In addition to the matching armour, the raven feathers on the clasps attaching her cloak to her breast plate marked her as a leader. She stopped a few feet in front of Raven and bowed. A thick braid of red hair slipped over her shoulders. "I'm Finna."

Though she didn't recognize the name, she nodded and waved her hands for Finna to straighten from her bow. "One of Cole's famed assassins."

Finna remained slightly bent at the waist, gaze cast down.

Maybe she didn't see Raven's hand waving.

"It is an honour to meet you again, mo bhanrigh," she said.

Well, now she was clearly an asshole. Raven lacked many skills, but memory wasn't usually one of them. The onslaught of event after event and the steep learning curve of learning her new role, though, meant less time for her to write things down. Besides a vague recollection, she couldn't recall the event where she met this warrior. That was what happened when they let someone with zero applicable work experience hold a position of power. Those characters in the books she read always magically morphed into perfect leaders, while she had to work hard every damn day just to keep up. To be mediocre. To keep what she had.

Through blood, sweat, tears and a lot of headaches, she'd wrapped her head around this role, but she still messed up. She still made mistakes and had flaws.

Frankly, she didn't trust anyone who claimed they didn't.

Raven used to write down all sorts of lists in whatever notebook she could find and recall the details on the lined pages with crystal clarity. At one time, she believed her inexplicable need to record information as a memory tool was just an odd personality tick. Then she discovered Odin's two ravens—Huginn and Muninn—combined, was her biological father. The same two birds who represented thought and memory. Suddenly, a lot of personality ticks began to make a lot more sense.

Sometimes life didn't allow her the time to make a list, either physically or mentally, though. She missed Cole. He'd always lean in and whisper names and important details to her. If he'd been here, she would've had this woman's entire backstory before she had a chance to kneel.

"The honour is mine," she said to Finna. "We're headed for Inari's court."

Finna finally straightened, her gaze flicked to Mike. "Would you like an escort?"

Mike bristled beside Raven.

"I have one," she said. What an odd question. The giant ginger scowling beside her wasn't exactly invisible or easy to miss.

Finna rocked back on her heels, her expression uncertain for the first time. "May I speak plainly?"

Oh dear. Conversations never went well when someone led with that. It was almost as bad as starting a sentence with, "No offense, but..." or, "Don't take this personally, but..."

She waved her hand for the assassin to continue. She wouldn't improve as a queen if she kept her head in the sand.

"My understanding of your little brother—"

"I'm not little." Mike pulled his shoulders back. He might've refused Rourke's unusual form of torture that he called training, but Mike worked out. In addition to being crafty, he was strong and capable. He just couldn't wield a sword and preferred to avoid fighting physically.

Finna cleared her throat. "My apologies. I'm still working on my English."

Raven almost snorted. Almost. Instead, she swallowed the sound down and choked on her own spit.

Finna didn't technically lie—she might very well

be working on her English—but most dark fae spoke the language fluently and from the lack of an accent, Finna fell into that category.

From Mike's deepening scowl, he'd caught the almost-lie as well and didn't appreciate it.

"Your younger brother is known for his mastery of human technology," Finna continued. "But that will not help either of you where you are going. Please reconsider and allow me to accompany you both."

"Thank you, Finna," she said. "Your concern and candor are appreciated, but I will continue with my brother."

Finna hesitated.

"Inari only allows one escort for visitors," Raven explained. If she showed up with more, she'd unnecessarily escalate the situation that didn't need any escalating. "And I require my brother's presence."

She didn't need or want the assassin's approval, but she also didn't want to dismiss her concerns. As Raven's feathers on her shoulders indicated, she'd risen to the position of Head Sentinel, a position of trust.

Finna didn't appear convinced.

"Our great-grandmother has no motive to harm us," she said.

Though Juni was right to exercise caution in revealing their connection with Inari, after going over her sister's meeting with the kami in fine detail, Raven realized keeping the secret was pointless. Inari had announced her relationship to Juni in front of her entire court. It was only a matter of time before the truth trickled down to the Underworld and the Shadow Realm.

Understanding eased away the tension on Finna' face. "I'd heard a rumour."

She leaned forward. "Next time you hear a rumour about me or my family in connection with any other fae, report it."

Finna jerked her chin up and down and thankfully knew better than to argue. Taking a large step back, she flung her arm in a flourishing motion to wave at the white portal. "Safe travels, mo bhanrigh."

Finna glanced at Mike.

Her brother responded with another patented scowl.

"And safe travels to your not-so-little brother." The sentinel stepped away, her cape fluttering behind her as she spun around.

Raven and Mike turned to the white portal of Inari's court.

"Looks like snow," Mike whispered.

It totally did. Juni described it as a whiteout flurry, and she'd nailed it. Raven pulled her shoulders back. "Let's go meet our great gigi."

"Please don't call her that again," Mike said right before she stepped through the portal to the realm of light.

No promises.

CHAPTER 11

"Just give me a second. I need to overthink this."

— RAVEN CRAWFORD

R aven stepped through the white portal only to discover the flakes weren't frozen at all. They were some sort of fragrant petal or shredded parts of petals—so many they appeared like a flurry of snow. The subtle smell caressed her senses while the soft petals skimmed past her skin. Calmness spread through her and she took a deep relaxed breath in.

Maybe she should go back and forth a few more times—just to see if the experience remained consistent.

"You can't play with the portal." Her brother's dry voice a foot away ruined the dream-like spa experience and for a brief second, she hated him. Didn't he know how much stress she carried in her shoulders?

Opening her eyes, Raven surveyed the white marble stonework under her feet and the fields of golden wheat on each side of the path that lay ahead. Gentle wind filled with floral scents teased the wheat, swaying the blades back and forth to give the illusion of a golden sea.

"Can you believe that sentinel?" Mike kicked a smooth pebbled down the marble path as they started to walk.

"What sentinel?" The Gathering Place was packed with them.

"The one who called me little," he grumbled.

"You need to get over that."

"Get over it? I haven't started whining yet."

"Could've fooled me." Interesting that Mike would get so hung up on one word when he knew the dark fae hadn't meant it that way.

Mike grumbled some more, but eventually they settled into companionable silence as they walked along the path. Soft rays from a white sun beamed down on fields of wheat which eventually gave way to cherry trees and rose bushes. When Raven and Mike crested a gentle slope, a white fortress came into view, rising above the trees in the distance at the end of the long path.

As they walked, their feet crushed the fallen pink petals from the trees and bushes, each step releasing tiny puffs of more fragrant air.

"This place gives me the creeps." Mike shivered.

"Would you prefer the aisle lined with skulls? Or perhaps you prefer Odin's decorating taste of weapons and battered shields taken from his victims and dead soldiers?"

Mike scowled. "At least dark fae don't pretend to be something they're not. One step in any of their lairs and you know they're rotten bastards." He waved at the petal covered path.

"You haven't seen Bane's cabin." And if she had anything to say about it, he never would.

"Bane's an exception."

She couldn't agree more.

"But this..." He waved his hand again at their surroundings. "This is deceptive, pure and simple. I don't care if Inari is our great-grandmother. Light or dark, a fae god is malevolent, not benevolent. This mystical, fairy-like glitter world is a façade. It's no wonder so many people falsely equate the light fae with good and the dark with bad."

Though he sounded a little jaded, Mike nailed it. The light fae had helped propagate their "wholesome" image and took advantage of it at every opportunity. In many ways, they were more duplicitous and devious than those in the other realms.

Raven gave up trying to talk sense into those regs

that fell for the fake image of the light fae long ago. "We can't save them all, hero. We're here to save Juni."

His cranky face softened briefly before turning into a hard mask. "Right."

They walked in silence along the path until they reached the bottom of the stairs that led into Inari's fortress. Up close, it looked more like a gigantic temple.

Mike peered up the steps and swore.

"This is what you've logged all that time in the gym for." She slapped him on the back. "I hope you didn't skip leg days."

"You know I didn't."

"Siblings don't let siblings skip leg days," she said absently as she continued to study the stairs. "Might be easier to shift. I'll meet you at the top."

"Raven, we're not meeting our great-grandmother for the first time naked."

"Well, I'll be clothed." She'd mastered the ability to shift and move her clothes to the shadow realm for when she reformed as a human. It had taken her a long time to perfect the skill, much to Cole's amusement and the maneuver still required a lot of her focus and intention. If she had to shift without warning or for an extended period of time, her outfit was as good as gone.

"That might be true, but you'll leave me on my own to climb these. I think it will look poorly on you. These stairs are made to make visitors pay for their visit in sweat. If you skip the entrance fee, you'll insult Inari."

Dang it, little bro was right.

"And even if Mom was raised to distrust the fae, she'll flay us alive if she finds out we didn't use our manners," Mike added.

The blood drained from Raven's face. Odin's dried twinkle berries. Queen of Corvids, mid-thirties and married, Mom still had the power to scare the bejeezus out of her. "You're right."

Without another word, she started up the stairs with Mike, one foot after the other, the gentle fragrant wind teasing her hair.

A famous Chinese proverb said the trip of a thousand miles started with one step. That might be true, but the wisdom did nothing to comfort Raven as she took each stair, pulling herself closer to her goal. This entry fee was enough to dissuade most people with any common sense from starting a war with Inari. Half the warriors would collapse before making it to the top.

Though more white than the yellow gold of Earth's sun, the roller sun packed a heated punch, bearing down on her and Mike relentlessly. About halfway up, she started to get light-headed. She wiped the sweat from her brow and continued methodically moving up the stairs.

Maybe she should've stuck with the battle bikini instead of the leather after all.

When Raven finally stepped onto the landing, she ignored the two kitsune guards standing at the entrance to the courtyard, staggered past statues and vomited in a large decorative vase.

"Rayray?" Mike stood somewhere behind her.

She held her finger up. The nausea swirling in her stomach hadn't stopped yet.

The hair hanging around her face disappeared as Mike collected it, holding the long black strands out of the way.

"Wouldn't want to meet our great gigi with puke in your hair," he said from somewhere behind her.

"Mom would kill—" The nausea hit again, and she cut her sentence off to empty her stomach. Her vision blurred and she swayed on her feet. Her heartbeat thudded in her ears as her overly-heated body clenched.

Mike rubbed her back and continued to hold her hair from her face. Crap. He'd never let her forget this.

When she straightened, he dropped her hair and stepped back. She wiped her mouth with her sleeve.

Well, now. That wasn't embarrassing at all. "We'll never speak of this."

Mike snorted. He'd definitely speak of it again. "Siblings don't let siblings live down embarrassing moments."

She sighed, accepting her fate of being the brunt of all jokes for the next few Roast Nights.

"Feel better?"

"Yeah. Heat, exercise and Bane-induced rage don't mix well for me apparently."

He chuckled and held out a stick of gum.

She snatched the offering from his open hand and peeled off the wrapping. "Where'd you stash this?"

"Vambrace."

"Nice." She popped the gum in her mouth and chucked the wrapper in the vase. As far as first impressions went, this wasn't a good start. The guards would report her actions to Inari.

Mike held out his arm. She hooked hers around his and held her chin up. She couldn't be the first person to lose their lunch after that climb.

The two kitsune guards scowled at them as they re-approached the entrance. Tall and centred in the way they stood and watched, the guards looked nothing alike, except for the bushy tails extending past their armour. They both had three tails which meant they were older than their smooth faces appeared and definitely more skilled than their relaxed postures indicated.

"Mike Crawford to see Inari." Her brother used his serious voice. The one she rarely heard since he hardly ever took anything seriously.

"Access denied," the kitsune with white hair on the left said.

Raven opened her mouth, but Mike's warning glance silenced her. They'd agreed to try for an audience with Mike's name first as Raven's might be met with a different reception.

"Denied specifically, or because my name's not on the list?" Mike asked.

"List," the guard's voice was clipped.

"Please inform Inari that her great-grandson humbly requests an audience," Mike said.

Both guards drew up at her brother's words. They glanced at each other and shrugged in unison. The other guard, the one with dark hair, spun on his heel and disappeared into the temple. His comrade retuned to doing his best statue impersonation.

Mike and Raven stood and waited. She didn't dare speak in front of the other guard, but the silence grated her nerves. At least she had a chance to catch her breath and cool down before standing before a kami.

A few minutes passed and the sound of armoured boots along the temple floor intensified before the second guard reappeared, his dark cheeks flushed pink.

"You may enter," he said.

Mike opened his mouth.

Before her brother had a chance to gloat, Raven elbowed him in the ribs. The guards would not appreciate Mike's particular brand of sarcasm. The one with white hair and cold blue eyes already looked ready to skewer them with his sword.

Mike shut his mouth.

"Our thanks." Raven dipped her chin at the guards and walked into the temple.

Mike followed and after they walked far enough

from the guards, he turned to her, his lip curled up in disgust.

"Our thanks?" Mike repeated her words with a mocking tone and moved his head side to side like one of those bobble head figurines.

"I don't look or sound like that," she said.

Mike smirked.

"Welcome to my temple." A melodious voice spoke at the end of a long pink runner and interrupted whatever snide remark Mike planned to say.

They both turned toward the voice.

A beautiful Japanese woman stood in front of a throne at the end of the path. Inari, kami of grains, harvest, and agriculture. A basket of woven grass sat to the side, overflowing with rice, and a white fox with four tails curled up at her feet. So far all of the kitsune had the typical red fur, not silver like Mike's fox form.

Silky hair as black as midnight contrasted with Inari's porcelain skin, and her eyes conveyed cunning intellect. And while her long lean body appeared willowy and fragile, she moved with delicate precision that hinted at deadly skill. If Inari ever deigned to fight, she wouldn't batter or smash. Like water moving past rocks, she'd flow around her opponents, slipping through their defences to cut them down without breaking a sweat.

Raven wanted to go home. Feeling inadequate and uncoordinated in the presence of her goddess great-grandmother might be understandable, but it still didn't feel nice. She was the Queen of Corvids, for Odin's sake. She couldn't afford to feel weak or insecure, let alone allow herself to look that way.

Ugh. Raven gave herself a mental shake.

So what if she looked like a drunk lumberjack compared to her gigi? So fucking what? She took a deep breath, pulled her shoulders back and marched on.

They finished walking down the aisle, ignoring the few temple guards and onlookers lining the path. A number of light fae milled around the sidelines. Some wore clothing from the Mortal Realm, but most opted for fae fighting leathers or armour.

"Thank you for granting me an audience. I apologize for arriving without invitation," Mike said before sweeping into a low bow that defied all the hours he spent in front of a computer screen.

"I couldn't pass up the opportunity to meet another great-grandchild." Inari inclined her head before she smiled, displaying perfect teeth, teeth so white they appeared to have their own lighting system.

"But I hadn't realized I would be meeting more than one. Greetings Branwen Camhanaich." The goddess turned to her and the sparkle in her gaze told Raven denying her identity would be a useless waste of their time.

Busted.

Now she definitely couldn't look or act weak. If

she'd remained some nameless plebe escorting Mike, that was one thing, but now she represented her court.

Raven nodded, conceding Inari's claim. She skipped the bow or courtesy, not out of disrespect but because her position didn't call for it. Fae were big on showing strength. Even though every instinct told Raven to show respect and deference to her ancestor, she locked her knees and remained stiffly upright.

Inari dipped her chin. "I'm doubly pleased today. Welcome to my court, Queen of Corvids."

"Thank you," she said. "Though I didn't come here on official business of my court."

Mike reached into his satchel and removed a bottle of sake. Cradling the bottle in both hands, near the base, he held the sake out toward Inari. "A small gift as a token of our thanks for granting us an audience."

Inari's smile widened and she plucked the bottle from Mike's hands. She turned and placed the sake on the armrest of her throne beside an orb that looked like a gold onion.

The hōju.

Juni had sent Raven pictures of the wish-granting gift, but her younger sister's description had been bang on. According to Juni, it was actually supposed to be a gold peach, not an onion. Made sense.

If Raven or Mike stole the hōju, would Inari still grant them a wish? Or cut off their heads?

One of the other reasons Mike led this party of two

was the hope Inari might bestow the same gift to him. Wishful thinking, of course, but worth a try.

"To what do I owe the honour?" Inari asked. "I doubt this is a social visit."

"Sadly, no. We'd like to discuss Juni's current predicament," Raven said.

Inari raised both her perfect eyebrows. "Last I saw your sister, she was healthy and safe. She used the hōju to heal a young, mortal man."

"And she bound herself to Bane as his caomhnóir," Raven said.

"Bane." Inari hissed. "Juni seemed like such a smart, young woman. Why would she do such a foolish thing?"

"To defeat your kitsune," Mike said.

"Which one?" She waved her hand at her courtroom as if all the light fae here were kitsune.

"Hikaru," Raven answered. "He was the one who trapped Juni and harmed the mortal man."

Inari waved her hand in the air again. "I'm not responsible for that. I denounced him as soon as I learned he tried to steal the hōju from Juni. He was one of my favourites but always held an ambitious streak. It fueled him to excel, to push himself harder and to achieve more compared to his peers, but it became his downfall as well, it appears. You can't steal a hōju. You need to receive it as a gift."

Well, guess that helped narrow down their options. It also explained why Hikaru hadn't killed Juni when he had the opportunity and tried to get her to hand it over instead.

"He tried to force her to give it to him," Mike pointed out.

Inari snarled. "If he weren't already dead, I would take care of him myself."

"Can you break the bond?" Raven blurted the question out. Dancing around a topic had never been her forte and she wanted Juni safe from Bane. Now.

Cole would've winced at her choice of words and Rourke would've hissed. Both would chastise her later for her lack of subterfuge. Now Inari knew exactly what Raven wanted and could use it as leverage.

Sure, Raven could've directed the conversation to Juni's situation eventually, maybe even manipulated a kami almost as old as dirt, but Raven doubted it. And she was just so tired of the fae games. So tired.

An image of the million stairs she had to hike up to get here streaked through her mind again. Maybe those stairs acted as more than just an entrance fee—they kept Inari's visitors at a mental and physical disadvantage. Smart fae god.

Inari's gaze sparkled. "Straight to the point, I see. I heard that about you."

"I don't mess around when it comes to those I love," she said. Oh dear, Cole would hate that she gave up this information as well. Really though, was it that much of a secret?

Inari considered her for a brief moment, a brief

moment that felt like it went on for days. "You may wish to learn to hide your emotions. Others may seek to use your weaknesses against you," Inari said, sounding almost exactly like Cole.

"You sound like my husband."

"*Beul na h-Oidhche gu Camhanaich* is wise and well-versed in the ways of the fae." Inari spoke Cole's full fae name with perfect inflection.

Pronounced roughly as "Bee-al nuh huhee-khye guh Ca-van-eekh," properly saying Cole's name had taken Raven a lot of practice. Everything "fae" took Raven time to master, something her husband and Inari would never quite grasp having grown up surrounded by the intricacies of the culture and language.

"Cole should be well-versed," she grumbled. He'd only had several human lifetimes to get things right.

Mike chuckled and shook his head.

"You would do well to heed his advice," Inari said.

"Normally, I do, but it's rather pointless right now. The whole Underworld is well aware of my family and my love for them. Those who would act against me have already tried to use my family. Bane does so as we speak."

Inari smiled again, but this time she didn't show her teeth and emotion didn't reach her eyes. "I can't break the sacred bond."

Raven's skin prickled and a numbness spread through her body. They came here expecting this outcome but expecting and hearing confirmation were two entirely different things. It had been a long shot, sure, but until Inari spoke those words, she still had hope.

And now the hope was gone. Her sister's prospects remained unchanged.

"Do you know of any way to break it?"

"No. That is why it's such a powerful connection. Only the holder of the bond can release the caomhnóir. Otherwise, death is the only way."

Not an option.

Team Crawford was back to the drawing board. If only Inari had gotten a hold of her rogue kitsune before he found Juni and Lincoln. If only Juni hadn't met him at all. If only, if only, if only...

"What exactly was Hikaru doing for you anyway?" she asked. "Juni told me she met him while she worked on a case."

Mike gave her a mean side-eye. Geez. He'd upped his game in the savage looks department. Next, she'd find out he'd been moonlighting as a runway model.

Inari smiled, the emotion still not reaching her eyes. "That, my sweet summer child, is none of your business."

The temperature in the room dropped. Her brother stiffened beside her and the sudden urge to be somewhere else, anywhere else, slammed into her. The spectators lining the aisle behind them stilled, the same people who pretended to converse with each other while they not-so-subtly eavesdropped.

Heavy silence settled on the courtroom and dread clamped Raven's spine. She needed to be careful. She had to select the right words and extract her brother from this situation. Obviously, she'd stepped on a line that separated acceptable questions from the insulting ones. She needed to tiptoe back to the side that wouldn't get her or her brother murdered.

"Of course," Raven said. "I didn't mean to overstep. We appreciate the time you've taken to meet with us. We will leave you now, if you wish."

Inari's dark gaze glinted, and she dropped the fake smile. "Until we meet again."

It took every ounce of self-control not to turn and run. Instead, Raven dipped her chin while Mike bowed before turning to leave the temple. They walked down the pink runner with their heads held high, and their backs exposed to a dangerous fae god.

The spectators watched them go, curious stares, blank stares, hostile stares. They all remained silent as they tracked her progress from Inari's throne.

Raven held her breath the entire time and waited for a knife to dig into her back. The death blow never came, but she didn't breathe properly until they reached the Gathering Place and she took Mike home.

The moment the crumbling pavement of the back alley behind their parents' place solidified under their feet, Mike pushed away from her, face still pale. "Let's never do that again."

She couldn't agree more.

"Do what?" A familiar deep voice spoke behind them.

Mike groaned and didn't bother turning around. Instead, he headed for the back fence gate. "I'll see you tomorrow."

Raven took a deep, measured breath, willing patience she didn't possess to magically appear. When she finally turned around, she found Bane exactly where she expected, wearing his shiny court armour and condescending smile.

Unperturbed by neither her brother's blatant dismissal nor her lack of enthusiasm, Bane smirked and sniffed the air theatrically. He stepped forward to flick a rose petal off her shoulder. "Family vacation?"

What the actual fuck. How'd he guess so easily?

He didn't, that's how.

Sure the rose petal may have been a giveaway, but only if he believed she travelled to the Other Realms. Flowers didn't exist solely in the Realm of Light, but Bane had eyes and ears everywhere. His spies must've sent him the news of their visit to Inari on some sort of magical speed dial.

"Were you hoping Inari would gift you with the hōju?" Bane examined his clean hand for dirt, purely for theatrics. "Hoping to banish me from your sister's life with a wish-granting peach?"

She glared at him.

"Or were you hoping to pimp out the Wish version of your twin?"

He better not be talking about Mike.

Bane leaned in and winked. "I'm talking about your baby brother, Mike. The resemblance is uncanny."

Don't kill Bane. Don't kill Bane. She curled her hands into fists and silently counted to ten. "What do you want?"

Bane lost his smirk. "Call off your dog."

"Excuse me?" They didn't have a dog, despite her serious hinting to Cole. He just shook his head exactly the same way as he did when she suggested miniature goats, hedgehogs or horses.

And a platypus. Those things were ridiculously cute.

"I don't have a dog," she said.

"You have Rourke. Remove him. He can't kill me and denying me access to my own guardian is futile."

Hah! So Bane had tried to snatch Juni away, and Rourke's presence was a deterrent. Rourke would be ecstatic to discover he was right. "I'll call off Rourke if you release Juni from the bond."

Bane snarled and threw down a lodestone. He disappeared in a swirl of angry red mist. Sure, she might've angered the mighty Lord of War, but damn it felt good.

CHAPTER 12

"We're so not hugging."

— MIKE CRAWFORD, TO ANYONE

After their visit with Inari failed to turn up any viable solutions or leads, Raven had to shift her focus, and right now, she really, really wished she'd chosen another option.

Mike hadn't stopped whining the entire time he trudged down the troll trail in his jeans and T-shirt beside Raven and Cole. At this point, she'd willingly learn dark magic for a mute spell to shut him up. It wasn't her fault they'd hit a temporary roadblock on freeing Juni. Nor did Raven have any control over when the cabin from the Kayden Smith case would be released. Nor was she to blame that it logically made sense for them to focus on Raven's missing troll prince in the meantime. At least they could work on something instead of waiting and twiddling their thumbs.

Cole had opted to join them on the trip to the troll kingdom. He said he wanted to spend time with her and found the possible slaughter of trolls who tried to betray her fairly romantic. He'd left the fae army with instructions to protect her family in their absence. Of course, he still insisted the fae army wasn't an army, solely based on his observation that the assassins made poor soldiers. When she asked him to give her an appropriate alternative, he faltered.

"Fine," he'd muttered. "It's an army."

She loved it when he deferred to her, even when she wasn't quite right, and she spent the rest of their night together showing him how much she appreciated it.

Currently, Cole stoically ignored most of the noise coming out of her brother as he walked alongside them in his black matte armour and matching cape that trailed him like a living shadow, but the tightness around his mouth and eyes hinted that even he, the paragon of patience when it came to her family, was also nearing the edge of his tolerance.

"Couldn't you just take Juni?" Mike asked for the umpteenth time.

"Really?" She stepped over a log and the long grass on the other side brushed against her boots. She'd opted for her formal queen attire for this outing. Her top, which resembled an armoured bra more than a breastplate matched bottoms that could only be described as a barbed chastity belt.

Cole had originally argued the outfit allowed for easier transformation while reminding her enemies and allies alike of her power. She didn't need full body armour. She'd never be in some epic battle where she could only wield a sword and shield. Instead, she needed to be light on her feet with unrestricted movement as well as shifting into her conspiracy.

Cole wasn't wrong, but it had taken awhile to get used to displaying so much skin. And she still suspected he had some sort of leather and strap fetish.

Mike sighed dramatically and continued to walk behind her.

"Look, I get that you'd rather sit behind your computer screen or solve your own case, but I need your nose and you need fresh air. You're so white you're turning translucent."

"Please don't try to spin this into something you're doing for me."

"You're right," Cole said, his lips twitching.

"See?" Mike jutted his hand out in Cole's direction. "Even Romeo agrees."

Cole didn't try to hide his grin. Only a Crawford would dare call the dreaded and deadly patron fae of assassins something as silly as Romeo.

"Of course, I agree. You're doing this for Raven so

she can rescue a troll child. Just as she will be helping you retrieve a missing human child. It's all about the children. Right, Mike?"

"I liked you better when you were doing that silent mysterious thing Rayray went all stupid over." Mike folded his arms across his chest and still managed to walk. "Besides, I also went to Inari's court for Raven."

Cole shook his head. "You didn't do that for Raven at all. You both went for Juni."

Mike snapped his mouth shut and went back to sulking. Honestly, what was up with him?

"What's the big deal?" Raven asked. She got hangry, Bear brooded, Juni turned into a hellion spit-fire at the slightest provocation, and her baby brother, Mike, got testy when he had to walk long distances on two legs. No one said the Crawford siblings were perfect, but this was more than Mike's aversion to two-legged walking. Something else bothered him.

"You've never kept score before and you used to track for cases all the time," she said.

"I just..." He cut his gaze away and took in the surrounding unspoiled forest. The troll domain had fresh, clean air, unburdened by the effects of the faepocalypse. A fast-moving stream of mountain run-off burbled nearby, and the path ambled through a grove of tall trees, though Raven suspected this trail had been made for goats, not human travellers.

"I'm not comfortable in my new form," he said.

"Because it's silver and Mom called it pretty?"

"I sprouted a second tail," he whispered as if he sat in a confession booth.

She bit down on her grin. That obviously upset her younger brother. She shouldn't laugh. At least not right now. Mike growing another tail didn't fit with her understanding of previous kitsune. They usually grew more tails with age and from that gained power. But what if it was the other way around? What if it was the increase in power that caused the growth of a new tail? An increase in power most often accrued over time.

The cause of Mike's extra tail didn't seem like the source of her brother's irritation, though, so she filed it away for later research.

"What's so bad about an extra tail?" she asked.

"I was out on a date when it happened."

"How in the Underworld did you fit in a date with all this crap?" Raven asked,

"Increased sex drive," Cole piped up.

"Ew." She shoved her husband's shoulder.

"There are some things my sister doesn't need to know," Mike grumbled.

Cole just shrugged and unsheathed a dagger to examine the tip.

"So what's the big deal?" Raven went back to the main topic. Maybe the conversation would help erase the last minute of talking from her brain. "You have two tails. So what?"

"So my date said it was the cutest thing she's ever seen."

Cole turned away with his dagger, but not in time to hide his grin or mask his chuckle. That didn't help at all.

"Let me get this straight." Raven shot Cole a pointed look before continuing. "You don't want to help save a child because you will have to shift into a fox and let your family—who loves you unconditionally, by the way—see your two tails? How were you planning on tracking Kayden Smith? Or does it have nothing to do with me and Cole and it's because we'll have a troll audience?"

"Ugh. Just forget it, okay?" Mike threw up his arms. "You make me sound awful and selfish."

She raised her eyebrows. She didn't want to dismiss Mike's feelings, but if she acted this way, he wouldn't hesitate to point out her poor attitude.

"That's because you *are* acting awful and selfish. If our positions were reversed, you would've told me this a lot sooner and with a lot less tact, so get that offended look off your face." She turned to jab him in the chest with her pointer finger. "There's a child missing. Suck it up, buttercup."

Mike grunted.

Raven stopped at the entrance of the troll's official territory, their wild magic pinging against her own. Like the extroverted friend in university, troll magic seduced by sheer enthusiasm.

"Why did we stop?" Mike asked.

Raven reached out with her corvid essence and

batted the intrusive magic away. She didn't have time or patience to deal with a power test.

The large boulder to their right shuddered.

Mike jumped back. "What the actual fuck?"

"Can't you sense them?" she asked and tapped her nose.

"Smells like forest—trees, rocks, moss, weeds. All the regular forest smells," Mike snarled. "And two annoying dark fae."

Okay, then. "No need to get snippy."

"You need to turn your shifter senses off for a moment," Cole said. "Embrace the fae."

"We're so not hugging," Mike said.

Cole took in a deep breath. The wind ruffled his cape behind him and made him look so out of place on a sun-dappled path in the middle of a forest. He should be standing on a hill overlooking the aftermath of a battle he'd won with the dawn sky behind him.

"I meant you need to use your newly released light fae powers to sense the trolls." Cole explained. "You need to push aside your shifter instincts until you understand your fae abilities because right now, you rely on the shifter stuff too much."

Mike's mouth dropped open. As someone who grew up in the shifter life, Cole may as well have told Mike to stop breathing.

"You now have access to your light fae powers. Even your fox form is showing signs of the kitsune," Cole said.

"Kitsune and fox shifters are not the same thing," Mike snapped.

"No, but now you're both. Or something else entirely. You need to turn your shifter brain off for a moment and let your light fae magic feel the environment," Cole said, with all the patience of someone who'd already had to train some people more dense and stubborn than Mike.

Specifically, her...she was "some people."

Raven almost felt sorry for her little brother. She'd barely survived Cole's lessons and these exercises had been the source of great frustration. *Almost* felt sorry. Then she remembered how much Mike had teased her, and that feeling of commiseration passed.

Right now, her brother looked like he needed to sit on the toilet. A tendril of bright magic spread a few feet from Mike before sputtering out. The power had been light and sparkly, like fairy dust, and nothing like the dark potent magic lurking in her veins. Maybe Cole's theory was correct. Maybe her dark fae powers completely overshadowed any light fae in her genetic make-up or it ate it like some sort of parasitic magical twin.

"Come on, Gingerbear. You can do it," she said.

Cole bit back a chuckle and failed, so it sounded like some sort of strangled cough.

"That's it. I'm locking your bank accounts." Mike pointed at her aggressively. "Again."

Luckily, she stored most of her wealth in a magical

vault with only one point of entry that was magically attuned to open only for her. He could lock her Canadian bank account to his heart's content, and it wouldn't harm her. It would, however, irritate and inconvenience her, which is why Mike threatened to do it.

"No, you won't," she said.

"Do you doubt me?"

"Not at all. I know you can, and you have, but this time you won't." Raven lifted her chin.

"Why's that?"

"One word."

He narrowed his eyes at her.

"Frey."

His eyes widened. "You wouldn't."

"Do you doubt me?" Frey had lived in her dungeons off and on for six years. She let him out periodically, but he always came back, intent on murdering her for the throne. He was due for another release soon.

Mike scowled. "If I didn't know better, I'd assume you were a cat shifter of some kind. It's not nice to play with your food. You should put that guy out of his misery."

Raven recoiled. Gross. "I have no intention of consuming Frey. And how *dare* you compare me to a cat shifter."

"If you guys are done with your squabbling," Iashi interrupted them. "I'd like to lead you to King

Tethaahin's castle so you can find the missing prince."

They turned in unison to find Iashi standing in the middle of the path with a troll guard on each side. She wore a similar outfit to the one from her court appearance. The supple brown fighting leather looked well-worn, moving with her easily. The boulder had disappeared, which meant Mike missed out on seeing them transform from rocks.

"This way." Iashi turned without waiting for a response and started walking down the path ahead of them. Her guards stood to the side and waited. After Raven, Mike and Cole passed them, they closed in and followed. Great, a troll sandwich with team Crawford as the bologna.

Cole continued to walk confidently with his cape billowing behind him. He looked like he'd cut down anyone who tried to harm them, and he would. Nothing seemed to faze him these days. If she ever saw him nervous or unsure, she'd know it was time to start freaking out.

Cole caught her stare and winked.

"What do you know about the troll tunnels?" Iashi asked over her shoulder.

"Only that the jotun have their own way of travelling between the realms since the beginning of time. Nerthach and Gwawrddur wanted me to resurrect a barrier so King Tethaahin could have a monopoly on inter-realm travel." She tried not to scowl when she spoke those two names, and failed. Her face twisted as if possessed by some demon and fueled by her resurfacing rage from her conflict with the trolls.

Iashi glanced over at Raven but kept walking. "I'm not sure how many fae would opt for that form of travel."

"Bane would." If it meant he could sneak his army into the Mortal Realm, he'd risk whatever the path required.

Which was something that never quite added up for Raven. Bane originally wanted a barrier so he could use the troll tunnels and take advantage of everyone else being stuck. In the end, Raven did what he wanted. Kind of. She'd erected a blockade, but she established the sentinels to monitor and regulate movement. Surely Bane could've worked with that and used the troll passageways as he originally intended.

As far as Raven could tell, though, Bane had abandoned that plan for world domination, because he'd walked into her court, used her sister as leverage and demanded she take everything down. Was it because her barrier allowed movement? Or had something else prevented him from enacting his previous masterplan?

An ugly thought crossed her mind, shocking and hard to ignore like a streaker at a soccer game. Maybe Bane still planned to use the tunnels. Maybe the missing troll prince played a part somehow. Maybe Bane needed Raven and Cole lured into the trolls' abyss filled with wild magic so he could launch his attack on the Mortal Realm.

She breathed through the instinctual dread that flared up like bad indigestion.

She'd had doubts about the trolls from the very beginning. The distrust came easily. But Cole had told her long ago, if she could get a troll to make a promise, it was just as secure as a fae oath. Iashi had promised safe passage and that she and the trolls were not involved with any sinister plot concocted by Bane. Raven trusted Cole more than she trusted the trolls.

"The Lord of War would be bold and brave enough to take our path," Iashi said. "But only because it would be a means to a bloody end."

That sounded ominous. "Okay."

The trail widened a little and Iashi dropped back to walk beside Raven, while Mike and Cole paired up behind them. "We refused him entrance into our lands."

Wait, what? That certainly explained why the Lord of War wasn't currently undertaking acts of war.

"The passage requires truth to oneself," Iashi continued as if she hadn't relieved years of worry with one sentence. "The troll tunnels are collectively referred to as Torghatten."

"Wait a minute." Mike frowned. "I looked that up. Torghatten is a mountain on an island in Norway in the Mortal Realm."

Iashi bobbed her head as she walked, lavender hair

swaying, leather outfit creaking. "That mountain is one of the entry points into the tunnels. A long time ago, a troll named Hestmannen made that entrance while he chased some reg woman around. When he realized she'd outsmarted him and he wouldn't catch her, he tried to kill her."

"Typical," Raven muttered.

Iashi smirked and continued. "King Tethaahin's ancestor, Sømna, intervened and threw his hat to block Hestmannen's arrow."

"A hat?" Mike's dry tone could wither prunes.

"Yes, his hat. Keep up, youngling." Iashi gave her brother a frown over her shoulder. "Still teeming with power from Ymir, the *hat* saved the reg woman and became the mountain with a hole in it." Iashi paused long enough to scowl. "And the location is constantly teeming with tourists who've heard the tale."

"You sound annoyed," Raven noted.

"You would be, too, if tourists restricted your movements. They make it hard to use the island as an exit because we never know who's hiking around the entranceway. It's infested with regs."

"And full of wild magic," Cole added. "The troll tunnels are ripe with it."

"Yes. Lots. And wild magic doesn't play well with others. Please keep your magic contained when you enter Torghatten." Iashi looked over her shoulder again at Mike.

Raven followed the troll's gaze and flinched. She'd

been so focused on Iashi and the information about Torghatten that she didn't notice her brother had surrounded himself with sparkling light fae energy while they walked and talked. Little bands of twinkling light fanned out and brushed against the surfaces and the stiff-walking trolls.

"Mike," she snapped.

"What?" He straightened.

"Stop that." She waved her hands at the magic tendrils. "You're feeling them up with your magic."

Mike gaped and without a word, his magic snapped back. The glowing aura around his body faded. The trolls surrounding them visibly relaxed, the tension in their backs easing away and their gaits lost their earlier stiffness.

"Sorry." Mike mumbled. "Their magic feels so different."

"Yes, but you need to ask permission before you play with other peoples' magic," Raven said.

He paled more somehow. "I didn't know."

"We're aware," Cole said, tone jovial. "Quite obvious."

Mike scowled and hunched his shoulders as he walked. They continued moving through the forest at a leisurely stroll. The gentle wind teased the leaves and birds chittered among the branches. The sun-dappled path before them continued to wind through the large tree grove.

"This isn't the way to Torghatten," Cole noted.

Raven stopped. The dirt crunched under her boots.

Iashi nodded. "I thought we'd take you to Tuguh's last known location to start the tracking."

In case Raven was wrong about trolls being involved. Iashi didn't say those words, of course, but she didn't need to. A look of grim hope twisted the ambassador's expression.

"Fine," Raven said. She didn't have the energy to crush Iashi's hopes and would welcome being wrong. The knot forming in her belly, though, told her this trip would reveal unpleasant things.

CHAPTER 13

"I learned long ago to let the Crawford siblings sort out their own disputes."

— COLE CAMHANAICH

At a distance, the troll castle appeared as a bare stone mountain rising from the surrounding forest. With jagged towers and crudely cut out windows, the fortress had been carved out of the mountain from the inside. Though it lacked the stonework spires and embellishments typical of European and fae castles, it held its own natural beauty. According to the historical texts in Cole's library, the jotun used their connection with nature and its wild magic to pull a giant slab of rock from the earth to mold it into the castle Raven now faced. The structure would've appeared like a natural protrusion if the village didn't surround the base. Raven wanted to see it from the inside.

Today was not that day.

Raven turned to Mike. "You're up, bro."

Her younger brother looked around and frowned. Their presence had drawn the attention of locals and a small crowd had gathered around.

"I can't shift here."

She raised an eyebrow. Shifters weren't generally shy about public nudity. Of course, he could, but he wouldn't. Mike wasn't like most shifters. He wasn't an exhibitionist. Stripping in front of a bunch of strangers would make him uncomfortable on the best of days. With a new fox form to reveal, he practically shook with unease.

None of that meant she wouldn't tease Mike. She was his sister, not a saint.

"Why not?" she asked, opening her eyes dramatically and batting her eyelashes.

Cole sighed and stepped forward. He pulled the shadows from the surrounding forest and buildings and manipulated them into bands. Without breaking a sweat, he wove the magic around Mike, until he formed an impenetrable wall of shadows. Mike now stood in the centre of a large, private shadowy cylinder. Raven called this skill the outhouse weave, because Cole made it for her when she'd had to pee in a sparse forest, and they had a guard detail with them.

Guess her husband was sick of listening to them bicker and solved Mike's problem on his own.

She blew Cole a kiss. His gaze sparkled with promises for later, and she felt the heat of his look down to her toes.

"Thanks," Mike mumbled from the other side of the shadows.

The troll onlookers leaned forward, trying to peer around them, presumably to see what happened to the ginger-haired man. The rustling of fabric should've given it away. Despite being shy, Mike excelled at dropping his pants with a moment's notice like all shifters. He wouldn't take long.

A high-pitch scream split the peaceful vibe of the forest. Raven jumped and called her scythe to her. The trolls stiffened. Some glanced around nervously and unsheathed their daggers.

At the same time, Cole dropped the shadow outhouse weave. In the center of the once enclosed area stood a white fox with two fluffy tails.

"Oh!" Raven banished her scythe and clapped her hands together. "You're adorable."

Mike darted forward and sank his teeth into her ankle. Pain streaked up her leg.

"Ow!" She shook her leg, but Mike held on. So vicious for such a cute thing. "Let go, you psycho."

Iashi froze beside Cole, her gaze shifting between

Raven and Cole and then back again. She'd promised Raven and her team a safe passage. Maybe this meant the troll owed her a favour now. Raven definitely didn't feel safe with Mike's fangs embedded in her skin.

Cole crossed his arms over his matte black breast-plate. The wind teased his cape and the black material fluttered against his armour and whispered on the ground. His lips quirked up at the corners.

"Are you going to help her?" Iashi asked the Lord of Shadows while Raven screeched and swatted at her brother.

"I learned long ago to let the Crawford siblings sort out their own disputes," Cole answered.

Mike snarled and finally released Raven's leg. Asshat. Blood trickled down the inside of her boot and a stabbing ache continued to throb near the wounds.

Raven stabbed Cole in the breastplate with her finger. "This is all your fault."

Cole chuckled and shook his head. "How is this my fault?"

"If you let me wear full fae armour, Mike would never have latched on like that." Technically, she dressed herself in the morning and she could've opted for armoured leather similar to the outfit she wore to Inari's court, but...leather was so warm.

And she couldn't resist an opportunity to poke at Cole.

"Let's not pretend I *let* you do anything, Einin." Cole's gaze smouldered and he stepped in. Now, less than a foot separated them, and their breaths mingled. Oh, he let her do plenty, and he knew it.

Raven had grown accustomed to his constant presence. So comfortable and safe with him that she often forgot how large and deadly he really was. Even now, with his sheer size acting as an intimidation tactic, she knew he'd never hurt her. The glint in his gaze told her he wanted to do a lot of things to her, with her, but harm was not one of them.

Who needed leather armour? With looks like that, Cole could keep her warm without even touching her.

Cole leaned down so their lips almost touched. "I was under the impression you were the Queen of Corvids."

"I am." She lifted her chin.

"Then you don't need my permission to do anything." He winked and straightened. "You can get your own armour any time."

She would've sputtered, but thankfully remembered they had an audience. The ambassador probably regretted asking them for help already.

Oh well. Iashi was stuck with them now.

Raven turned around and found Mike sitting down and cleaning his hind paws. He bared his teeth at her, some still stained with her blood.

"If you're done with the juvenile tactics, let's go track down the missing child," she said.

Mike whined before bolting ahead of them. His bushy tails whipped against her legs.

"So cute and fuzzy," she whispered.

Cole chuckled. "He really will mess with your bank accounts if you keep this up."

"Worth it." She watched her brother approach Iashi in his little fox body with his little, fluffy paws, tufted ears, and his puffy tails. "Do you think he'll let me pet him?"

"Do you want to keep all your fingers?" Cole asked.

Yeah, he had a point there.

When Mike sat in front of Iashi, she pulled a shirt from a sealable bag and held it out for him to smell. Presumably, the clothing belonged to the troll prince.

Mike sniffed the shirt with his ears pinned back. He swiveled around and lowered his nose to the ground. Taking in alternating short and long breaths he snuffled along, popping his head up to scurry a few feet ahead only to halt and snuffle along the ground like a truffle-detecting pig.

The moment he picked up a clear trail became evident to anyone well-versed in fox body language or her brother. His ears and tails snapped up. Mischief danced in his gaze—not because he was up to no good, but because foxes always looked like they planned to enact mayhem when they set their minds to something. She'd known Mike his whole life. He always looked like that when he found something interesting.

"He's got something," she whispered to Cole.

Her husband perked up, hand slipping to his

sword. A gleam of anticipation sparked in his gaze, but for completely different reasons.

"No stabbing people," she reminded him.

Cole scowled.

"At least not right away. Let me question them first."

He narrowed his eyes, but her words seemed to placate him, and the glint in his gaze returned. Honestly, dark fae and their need to stab things might be the death of her one day.

Mike scampered forward, occasionally snuffing the ground and snorting. They followed, but not too closely. She didn't want their familiar scents to overwhelm the one Mike tracked.

He darted forward and they picked up the pace. Now that they had moved farther from the common area, the trail would be easier for Mike to follow.

Iashi glanced at them as they jogged after the fox, her thin lips curving down and emotion pinching at her expression.

Raven had no idea where Mike took them, but one more glance at the troll ambassador told her Iashi knew and wasn't happy about it one bit. That narrowed the options down to one.

They turned the corner on a path winding through the trees and watched Mike's cute, fluffy tails disappear down a trail through a darker section of the woods. Unlike the earlier one that gave off a light fairy feeling, with open spaces and dappled sunlight, this section of dense evergreens provided the opposite. The trees surrounding the trail had grown together to block out the sunlight and gnarled branches reached over the path as if begging for help from the heavy strands of lichen hanging from their bark.

Mike had definitely taken the road less travelled by.

Would it make all the difference?

She snorted and pushed some of the Old Man's Beard out of the way to continue down the path.

Cole turned to narrow his eyes at her. "Did you just make some witty comment to yourself?"

She pressed her lips together and focused on jogging without tripping over the gnarled exposed roots criss-crossing the path ahead of her. "I don't know what you're talking about."

His smirk called her a liar better than any words.

Mike skidded to a halt a few feet down the trail and glanced over his shoulder at them, his tongue flopping in and out of his mouth as he panted.

"Cool your jets, speedy. The scent isn't going to go cold that quickly," Raven called out.

Mike flashed his teeth at her, again.

A shadow spread over his body. Not a shadow cast from their group, but something or someone else.

"Mike!" She reached out with her hand.

Branches snapped and the trees groaned as a massive figure made for nightmares emerged from the tree cover. With arms stretched out toward Mike, the ogre lunged. The fox dove under a bush, slipping away from the ogre's grasp. The beast stumbled forward, each step thundering on the ground. He regained his footing and snarled at the bushes.

Inhumanly tall with disproportionately huge heads, ogres had strong bodies corded with muscle and were the official giants of the supernatural community. Sparse hair sprouted in irregular patterns over their scalp, making ogres perpetually appear to be going bald, regardless of gender or age.

This ogre was no exception, fitting the stereotypical descriptions like a cover model for an ogre magazine. He wore large swaths of dirty, ripped fabric to cover his genitalia, and had the typical blue-gray skin tone and naturally scowling expression. All ogres had a sickly appearance, at least by reg and fae standards. That explained why the majority of myths told stories of ogres eating children. Ogres ate meat, but they'd just as likely consume a deer as a child. They viewed all animals—humans included—as an acceptable food source.

The ogre turned to Raven and her comrades and bellowed. Maybe that was the ogre equivalent to a dinner bell? She turned to Cole.

Her husband looked positively gleeful.

Seriously. Why was this her life?

She called her scythe and sunk her magic into the weapon, letting its power dig in and grip her psyche. The weapon's essence melded with her own just as more freakishly large bodies charged out of the forest, aiming straight for them. Trees toppled over and thudded to the ground, blocking the path ahead.

Iashi cursed and spat off to her side. The troll ambassador drew her sword and jerked her chin at the two other troll guards. They looked even less pleased to be here, which said a lot.

The ogres lumbered toward them, each heavy footstep shaking the ground. The still-standing trees groaned, their branches shaking and the leaves rustling. Instead of the ogres brandishing the large, barbed clubs they were known for, they carried nothing at all. That didn't make them any less danger-ous. Their giant hands were weapons all on their own.

Cole drew on her power and she opened the bond connecting their souls. Her corvid essence fused with Cole's, giddy for the opportunity to play with his power.

She swung the scythe in her hand, power slashing out from the blade and crashing into the ogre closest to her. He snarled and stumbled, but momentum and sheer determination kept him moving forward. If he fell on her, he'd crush her. There was no surviving that.

Raven dove out of the way, tucking her chin and rolling. She sprung to her feet and spun, quickly checking on the rest of the group. Cole hadn't moved, opting to wrap his shadows around his opponent, again and again, until the beast looked more like a pig in a blanket than a fearsome supernatural being from her mom's twisted bedtime stories.

He could've demolished all three ogres on his own, using his shadows as deadly blades. Evidently, he refrained to allow her an opportunity to practice. As for the trolls, her husband probably wanted to gauge their skill level while keeping the extent of his abilities secret.

Even in the face of danger, her husband made calculated decisions.

The three trolls dashed around the third ogre, shockingly agile. Trolls usually hobbled around and gave the impression they weren't nearly so nimble. Having fought a retinue of trolls before, Raven had already experienced their capabilities first-hand, but seeing it again still managed to surprise her.

The trolls continued to dance around the other ogre, weaving their wild magic around him while they slashed at the vulnerable belly skin. He roared, shaking the gnarled trees with his ferocity.

The ogre who charged at her had finally turned his large, lumbering body around. He stomped at the ground and fumed.

Honestly, was she supposed to bring a red cape or something? That guy knew he was an ogre, not an actual bull, right?

Before she had the chance to question him or try to deescalate the situation, he dropped his chin and barrelled toward her again.

"Stop toying with him." Cole had wrapped up his tussle with the enemy and now stood to the side with his arms crossed. He always stood in a way that exuded relaxed confidence, like nothing would faze him, nothing would prove too difficult to take care of. If a swarm of wild banshees rushed them from the forest right at this moment, he'd take care of them with quick, calculating efficiency.

The ogre barrelled toward her. She gathered her power, embraced her corvid essence, and let her consciousness split into hundreds of birds. Her conspiracy erupted from where she once stood. Like a hive mind, she controlled the massive group of ravens as an extension of her mind. Each bird carried her true essence, but if the ogre managed to kill a bird, instead of losing a piece of herself, her consciousness would simply redistribute to the rest of the conspiracy.

The ogre stumbled and stopped where she'd disappeared. His head snapped up to snarl at the birds.

Gripping her magic and pulling on Cole's, Raven called for her scythe and clothes. In midair, she reformed, fully clothed, gripping her weapon. She swung the scythe, slashing through the ogre's thick skin and bones to sever his head from his body.

The decapitated head fell to the forest floor with a loud thud.

Raven landed a few feet away, still holding her scythe. The ogre's body toppled over and crashed into the nearby trees lining the path.

"Show off." Iashi knelt by the third ogre's body to use its loin cloth to clean her sword.

Cole grinned at Raven. Lust and pride pulsed through the anam cara bond connecting them. He wanted her. If they didn't have an audience, she'd pounce on him and let him have his way with her right here on the forest floor.

She glanced over at the decapitated corpse.

Okay, maybe not *right* here.

Cole released his hold on her power and the magic wailed as it retreated back to her through the bond. Her magic was drunk on Cole's, having become addicted since the first taste.

"Such a waste," Raven said to no one in particular. "The ogre population is critically low, isn't it? They just lost three prime males. Why would they risk it?"

"Their numbers are critically low because they consistently make poor life choices without considering the consequences," Cole said.

Iashi waved at the other dead body at her feet. "Case in point."

Raven sighed and opened her mouth to say more, that loss of life was still sad, even if they had no choice in defending themselves.

Cole shook his head, the movement brief and subtle. He couldn't technically read her mind, but he read her face and knew her well. He didn't need to tell her to stop talking, not with words. She could read his expression just as well as he could hers. He didn't want her to reveal her compassion because others would view it as a weakness, even if it was one of her personality traits he adored.

Raven bit back her words and bared her teeth. She could ignore Cole's advice, of course, because that's what it was—advice, not an order—but she knew he was right. Fae had an unhealthy obsession with weakness and avoiding it at all costs.

She opened her mouth, not quite sure what she wanted to say, but knowing it had to do with orders and their bed. A streak of white in the forest ahead distracted her, though, and she shut her mouth.

Mike sat his cute, fox butt on one of the fallen trees in the centre of the path up ahead, swishing his two fluffy tails behind him with impatience. Sunlight broke through the hole in the tree canopy and bathed him in its golden light, making him glow.

"We're coming," she called out to him.

He huffed and sprang to his feet, jumping off the fallen tree and disappearing to the other side before Raven had a chance to stretch out any of her muscles.

Bastard.

Without a word, the trolls sheathed their weapons and straightened, while Cole moved to walk beside her. After climbing over the trees strewn across the path, they followed the sly fox into the shadows. The path wound through the silent forest of gnarled trees until it dipped over a steep-sloped hill.

"What exactly am I looking at?" Raven asked.

"Torghatten," Cole said. "Or more specifically, two of its many entrances."

The path descended a steep embankment and branched off, disappearing into two identical caves. The opening to each unknown abyss sat below a fast-flowing river, which meant the two tunnels ran under raging water.

Awesome.

Neither tunnel appeared to have an exit on the other side, either.

"You said you've travelled this way before?" She peered up at Cole. Though she knew her anam cara intimately, she still discovered new things about him every day. He didn't intentionally keep information from her "for her safety or best interests" anymore, but he'd lived a long fae life. Sometimes he just forgot things he did or places he'd been until it became relevant to the situation.

A troll guard stood outside each of the tunnel entrances, and they straightened as Raven and her party approached.

Raven turned to Cole. "Where do each of the caves lead?"

He shrugged. "It changes. Only the troll guards know."

"I feel like I've heard this somewhere before." She frowned and rifled through her memories but couldn't find what she searched for.

"It's a mortal realm riddle," Iashi said, her tone implying how distasteful she found it.

"The riddle begins with you dying and finding yourself in front of two doors. One leads to heaven and the other to hell," Cole prompted.

She snapped her fingers. "That's right. And there are two identical trolls in front of each door. The instructions say you can only ask one of the trolls a question," Raven said, recalling the memory of one of Mom's stories.

Cole grinned. "That's right. And one troll will always lie to you and the other will only tell you the truth. The trolls themselves know which one lies and which one is honest, so what do you ask and who do you address your question to?"

Raven didn't care where the entrances led, she just wanted to know which one was taken by the people responsible for kidnapping Prince Tuguh.

She glanced down at Mike. He whined and rubbed his nose with his paw. He'd stopped right where the path forked and his fox equivalent to sign language said he'd lost the scent.

Raven narrowed her eyes at the two guards and marched over to the one on the right.

"A troll travelled this way about four weeks ago with cargo or a bag large enough to contain a troll child. If I ask the other troll which entrance this traveller took, which entrance will he point to?"

Raven would take the tunnel the troll didn't point

at. If he were the troll who told the truth, he'd know the other troll would point to the wrong cave. If he were the lying troll, he would lie and say the honest troll would point to the wrong tunnel. In both cases, regardless of which troll stood in front of her, he'd point to the tunnel she didn't want to take.

Nailed it.

Cole laughed somewhere behind her. "What are you doing?"

Both of the troll guards scowled at her.

Iashi stepped forward to stand beside her. She normally looked as though she'd eaten something sour, but somehow the ambassador's expression had morphed to deepen her grimace, showing disappointment and disgust. "That's a silly mortal realm riddle. These two tunnels lead to the Realm of Light and the Underworld, not heaven or hell. And neither Earl nor Samantha are consummate liars."

Okay...Raven was an idiot. She offered a sheepish smile, but the troll ambassador wasn't having any of it.

"And you're travelling with me," Iashi continued to growl. "You don't need to trick them into answers."

Wow. She'd really managed to offend the ambassador. Crap. She finally had a chance to test out her answer to a childhood riddle and it totally backfired.

"My apologies," she mumbled. "I didn't mean to offend."

Iashi replied with a curt nod before turning her

attention to the tunnel. "Sam, which tunnel did the traveller take?"

"Travellers," Sam replied in a low craggy voice. "There were three travelling together and they took my tunnel. We noticed they had a large bag with them but didn't hear or see anything suspicious. We would've reported them otherwise."

"Did you recognize them?" Iashi asked.

Both guards shook their heads. Drat.

"And where does your tunnel lead?" Raven asked.

"The Gathering Place."

CHAPTER 14

"Nothing and no one is infallible."

— SENTINEL, SPOUTING WISDOM

"**M**o bhanrigh." The sentinel knelt before Raven, head bowed, posture tense. The guild assassin resembled all her dark fae warriors and this shift of guards looked almost identical to the last group she'd met when she travelled to Inari's court with Mike. The sentinel held himself like a trained fighter, which he was, had an emotionless expression that said he'd kill the enemy without remorse, which he would, and he radiated sexual allure to match his attractive features. They all looked like that.

Raven still couldn't quite grasp why there weren't more half-fae bastards like herself running around the Mortal Realm. When she'd asked Cole, her anam cara had shrugged and explained the fae had lower fertility rates to balance out their long, life spans. Pregnancies were rare. If they decided to start a family, they'd have to mentally prepare for it to take a long time.

Totally fine with her.

Raven wasn't in a hurry to bear any crotchfruit into the world. She loved helping with her younger siblings and watching them grow up, but she had no intentions of entering the sleep-deprived, caffeine addled, stress-inducing, guilt-riddled world known as motherhood anytime soon.

Mike shot forward, nose to the ground, and paced around the courtyard.

The Gathering Place acted as a lobby to the Realm of Light and hadn't changed since her last visit. The floating island of white slab stones still held the portals to all the different courts within the Realm of Light. The Gathering Place wasn't truly an island, of course, but it was heavily shielded and held apart from the Other Realms.

Mike currently sniffed around the base of a portal to Inari's court. The memory of scented petals whispering across her face caressed her mind. Maybe she could quickly pop over and come back.

Mike shook his head and darted to the next portal.

Raven sighed and waved at the sentinel to stand.

He continued to stare at her boots, though, so he didn't see her gesture.

"Rise, sentinel," she said.

He rose to his feet, all grace and no scramble. When his dark gaze met hers, the irises bled out making both eyes appear completely black. Someone felt amorous in her presence.

Cole growled from where he stood beside her.

The sentinel snapped straight and dropped his gaze to her boots again.

Great. Cole's over-protectiveness might be sweet, if not a little frustrating after so many years together, but it also impeded her ability to garner information. Cole lacked tact and they fundamentally disagreed on how best to interrogate someone. Raven insisted fear made the target clam up, where Cole was adamant it freed their tongues.

Right now, the sentinel glanced over at Cole and remained stiff where he stood in front of Raven.

"About four weeks ago, a young troll child was taken from King Tethaahin's castle. We followed the path of the trolls here." Well, not entirely true. They didn't go through the creepy troll tunnel because they knew the destination and skipped ahead.

"There's an embargo on troll travel," Raven continued.

Iashi grumbled behind her.

Yeah, Raven was still salty Nerthach and Gwawrddur tried to kill her and even angrier about how the trolls' interference nearly cost Juni her life. Raven refused to apologize for it, but maybe, just maybe, she could ease the restrictions.

Raven kept her focus on the sentinel in front of her. "I didn't receive any reports of altercations with trolls from here, though, so help me understand. Did a troll have a pass? Is it possible they used some sort of shielding or glamour to slip past? Did someone take a bribe?"

The sentinel shook his head at each question. "We didn't have any altercations with trolls while I was on shift. We have staggered rotations, so the likelihood of a fight breaking out and none of the sentinels reporting it is unlikely. The same reasoning applies to bribes."

"Unlikely, but not impossible," she said.

He shook his head. "Not impossible. Nothing and no one is infallible, but we all appreciate our new roles and swore a fae oath to you. The possibility we all somehow broke it without detection and were all on the same shift at the same time seems beyond probable."

"What about passes?" the troll ambassador asked.

"No troll possesses a pass to the Realm of Light. No troll has dared to step foot in the Gathering Place since the sentinels took our positions unless they were accompanied by a fae guard."

"Any of those?" Cole asked. "Escorted trolls?"

"None. I'll ask the other sentinels, but we record

any special travellers and report them to you. You would've already heard about it."

Which is how she found out her sister had travelled to the Realm of Light with a kitsune escort before Lincoln gave his report. Honestly. Where did Juni get that attitude from? Stubborn mule.

"So no trolls," Raven said.

"No trolls."

"At all."

"You can keep asking the question in different ways," Cole interjected. "But I don't think the answer is going to change."

The sentinel standing in front of her sighed in relief, but she ignored him, her mind already scrambling to make sense of the information. If the trolls never popped out on this side of the tunnel, where in the Underworld did those fuckers go with the kid?

"Mike?" She looked down at her brother who sat at her feet in fox form. "Did you pick up the trail?

He whined and dropped his head. Drat. The trolls had blocked their scents and that of the prince's by the fork before Torghatten, but normally, scent blockers only worked within a certain radius unless they all possessed extremely expensive scent-blocking charms. Given Mike had successfully tracked the abductors from the village to Torghatten, she ruled out the latter possibility.

Yet, none of their scents were in the Gathering place. Either they blocked their scents again, or...

She looked over her shoulder at Cole. "They handed the prince off to someone else in the tunnel."

Cole nodded, expression grim.

Crap.

In order for Mike to learn the new scents of the people who picked up the boy in the tunnels they'd have to travel through the wild magic death trap known as Torghatten.

Raven's stomach twisted. "We have to go back."

CHAPTER 15

"At this point, I'm about 98% feral and will not integrate back into society successfully."

— UNKNOWN, BUT ALSO RAVEN

The gaping maw of the tunnel filled with wild magic stared back at Raven. If she had a choice, she'd hop right out of here. The erratic power licked at her skin like the blistering warmth from a campfire. Little pricks and sizzling snaps of heat followed by damp cold.

She turned to Cole. Maybe they could track the abductors another way.

He glanced down at her, face grim. "We have to go in."

"You swore you couldn't read my mind."

"Didn't need to."

She sighed and turned back to stare at the tunnel some more. Nope. Still freaky. She *knew* the troll passageway wasn't a living entity, not capable of conscious thought, but the air around the entrance vibrated as if Torghatten laughed at her.

Though she had troll guards standing behind her and her anam cara beside her, they did little to settle the unease flittering along her spine.

Mike whined and pressed against her leg. She'd prefer to pick him up and hold him tight, with his fur tickling her nose, but she needed her hands free. And realistically, Mike was better off on the ground. Quick and sly, he had a better chance of survival by ducking away and darting off into the sunset instead of being coddled by his older sister.

"Let's do this." She gripped the scythe in one hand and let its potent energy vibrate through her arm. At one time, she'd found the power overwhelming, now it comforted her.

They entered the cave.

She paused and listened for a death knell.

Nothing.

She peered into the shadows, waiting for the boogeyman to leap out.

Nada.

She stood in the dark entrance and breathed in the damp air waiting for something to happen. When nothing did, she turned to Cole to say something, but his tense muscles and grim expression told her he knew something she didn't.

Pffft. Story of her life.

"Remember," Cole said. "Jotun magic can't be controlled, only seduced."

Yeah, okay. "A little more explanation would be nice."

"The fee is usually something small like a prick of blood. It's hard to explain or anticipate Torghatten's wild magic, though. It's one of those things that becomes clear when you're experiencing it and no amount of preparing beforehand will make a difference. Whatever you do, don't use your magic or shift."

She glowered.

"We will be okay, Einin."

But he wasn't one hundred percent sure. Danger existed when travelling these tunnels and while he must've figured the risk low, there was still a risk. He never said it, but the tension around his shoulders spoke for him.

"You are my light." Cole reached out and tucked an errant strand of hair behind her ear. "I'll never let anything happen to you."

They continued to walk into the cave, their booted footsteps echoing down the rocky corridor. Tiny microbes illuminated the dark tunnel with their bioluminescence. The magical effect mimicked a starry night and an urge to skip tingled her legs.

Skip.

Her.

In a magical troll tunnel.

Raven stopped and shook her head. Thin needles of magic fell from her skin. Wild magic. Jotun magic.

As if dipping its toes in unknown water to check the temperature, the thin wisps of power reached out to get a taste of her. Raven's shadow magic and corvid essence surged up, bursting through her skin, ready to answer the magical equivalent to a knock on the front door.

Raven tightened her grip on the scythe and used every ounce of control to prevent the power from opening the flood gates. Still a rookie in fae magic, she had a lot to learn about the capabilities and limits of her power. Navigating unknown territory was not the time to take a side-quest into self-discovery.

Power vibrated through the tunnel. Like water breaking through a dam, it rushed forward, threatening to drown them all. The wild magic got its lick and wanted more.

"Brace yourself," Cole said.

The erratic magic danced around her, flicking her hair, pinching her skin.

Come play, the magic whispered. *Come dance with us.*

"I'd love to, but I'm a little busy."

The magic whirled around her faster. The hair

whipping turned to hair pulling, the skin pinching changed to painful slaps.

Dance with us, a lyrical voice teased her senses as the wild magic continued to play with her, painfully.

"What do I do?" she turned to Cole.

He'd disappeared.

She spun around. Everyone was gone. The entire tunnel was empty. Except her and the magic.

Let it go, the power whispered. *Let it all go and be with us*.

She clenched her free hand into a fist and called her power. If this magic wanted to dance, she'd dance with it all right. She'd rain down all the might of the Corvid Court and obliterate this devious, meddling pull. She gathered her corvid essence from within, building it and weaving in the shadow magic that came with her mantle and bond with Cole.

Cole.

Her anam cara's words from earlier whispered through her mind as if he stood behind her and spoke in her ear. Wild magic couldn't be controlled, which meant it couldn't be contained or conquered.

It could only be seduced.

Raven froze, letting her power fall away from her control. If she tried to fight this magic head on, she'd lose. All her power would get lost with the wild magic. Cole's words made sense now.

At least the first part.

How did one "seduce" a magical power?

"You want to dance?" she asked.

Yes. Dance. Dance with me. Feel the caress of power.

Raven shrugged. If this wild jotun magic wanted a dancing partner, so be it.

"If I dance with you, will you allow me and my party safe passage?"

Yes. Yes. Safe. As long as you do no harm. Its lyrical voice echoed through the tunnel.

Where was everyone else? Were they off in another reality doing their own seducing, or had the tunnel transported them someplace else so it could pick on her in private? What had the magical power done with them? With Cole? Was he safe? She had to assume he was okay, or she'd never get through this trial.

Raven leaned the scythe on the rocky wall of the cave before letting the wild beat of the magic's rhythm take over. The music caressed her as she moved her hips along with the sway of the breeze. A raspy hum vibrated in the tunnel, bouncing off the rocky walls to surround her. The beat wove through the air, rhythmically thumping along to her heartbeat. She continued to move, swaying with the wild music, and accentuating each turn and swing of her hips to play with the sensuous undertones of the new sounds.

Yes, dance.

Raven lost herself to the music, no longer caring how she looked. She danced as if Cole stood in front of her and she had to show him how he made her feel. Her skin vibrated with the music. Her heart beat to the drums, her feet moved along the path of the ancient jotun ancestors. Each step sent magic fluttering up from the rocky ground.

And just as the music steadily increased, it left the same way, fading until Raven stood alone in the silent tunnel, short of breath but invigorated.

Thank you, the magic whispered, slipping off her skin like a goodbye kiss.

Someone whistled behind her.

She spun around to find Cole, Mike, and her entire troll escort. They appeared completely fine and though they weren't out of breath like her, they wore a range of expressions.

Mike lay on his belly, snout buried under his paws and whined, while the trolls looked amused, as if they just watched an entertaining train wreck and didn't know what to make of it.

And Cole...

Her anam cara watched her with a wild gaze. His posture tense, his breathing heavy. Heat radiated from their bond. If they didn't have an audience, he'd have her naked and wrapped in his arms pushing inside to claim her with each thrust of his hips. That smouldering gaze said it all.

She walked over to him slowly.

He remained frozen, watching each step like a predator tracked its prey.

"Did you like what you saw?" she asked, wrapping a tendril of her hair around her finger.

"Very much." His voice was raspier than usual, lower.

She smiled.

He leaned forward.

She smacked him on the arm. Not hard, more like a love tap.

He straightened and frowned at her. "What in the Underworld was that for?"

"For not telling me I'd have to get frisky with jotun magic to seduce it."

His mouth dropped open.

"At least it only wanted to dance. What did you have to do? Hump it?" The idea made her inextricably angry. Okay, not inextricably. She knew why. Jealousy was an awful emotion, and it twisted her stomach like a wet towel being wrung out to dry. Growing older didn't exempt her from this feeling, either.

"I travelled this passageway a long time ago," Cole said, his dark gaze scanning her face. "I was only asked for a drop of blood. I did not expect that."

I would never ask you to bleed for me, whispered the magic. *Women bleed enough, body, mind, and soul.*

The wild magic had a point.

She narrowed her eyes at Cole, and he held his hands up in defence. "I'm telling the truth."

"He is." Iashi decided to chime in. "That's the

usual cost of admission. A dance is an unusual
request."

She squeezed her eyes shut. "Did you all get to
watch the show?"

The troll's mouth cracked open to a wide smile of
jagged teeth. "Front row seats."

Mike whined again.

"Sorry, bud." There were some things brothers
shouldn't have to see. Their older sister gyrating to
soundless music was definitely on that list.

"Do you have the scent?" she asked Mike as she
retrieved her scythe, hefting its familiar weight in her
hand. They didn't have to dwell on her dancing skills,
and Cole needed to shift his focus quickly before he
tried to use his magic and whisk her away to somewhere private.

Mike popped up and sauntered ahead. Guess that
was a yes.

Cole gripped the back of her arm, just above her
elbow before she could follow. He leaned down and
whispered, "When we get home. I want you to dance
for me."

She leaned back into the heat of his body. His
other hand slipped around her waist and held her, his
hand splayed over her stomach. He dropped his head
into the crook of her neck and dropped a kiss on the
sensitive skin.

"That dance was for you," she said.

"You drive me wild." His desire tugged at the bond

between them. Normally, he kept a tight leash on his emotions, not wanting to drown her with his intense feelings.

If she was getting this from him now, it meant lust and need overwhelmed him. She smiled slowly and arched into him, her butt rubbing against his groin.

He cursed and stiffened against her. All of him stiffened. He nipped her earlobe. "Minx."

"Pffft. I'm a raven, not a rodent." She pushed off him and followed her brother down the cavernous tunnel.

The trolls chuckled and moved to follow Mike, while Iashi came up to walk beside her, amusement tugging at her thin lips. She raised her hands to grip the same triangular pendent she'd worn to the Corvid Court. Up close, the single rune etched in silver was easier to make out.

Iashi glanced over and caught her staring. "A gift from the king. It means loyal. Every member of King Tethaahin's household wears one as a reminder of our oaths."

Raven nodded and they continued to walk, each lost to their own thoughts.

"Why would the magic ask me for a dance instead of blood?" she asked the troll ambassador.

Iashi shrugged. "Wild magic is unpredictable. Maybe you were randomly selected or maybe..." She glanced at Raven and frowned.

"What?"

Iashi shrugged again. "It's rumoured the wild magic of Torghatten will only take what the traveller can bare to give. Maybe it felt you couldn't afford a drop of blood."

"And I could afford the humiliation of a dance?" Raven huffed.

The ambassador's lips twitched again.

The first explanation made no sense. There was enough blood rushing to her groin right now from her interaction with Cole to reject that possibility. "There must be another reason."

Luckily, Iashi didn't shrug again. Raven could only handle so much ambivalence when it came to ominous powers that could drastically affect her life. Not knowing things had already proven a weak shield against her enemies in her role as the Corvid Queen. Ignorance wasn't bliss, it was death.

Why had the wild magic treated her differently? Being odd among regs in the Mortal Realm was one thing. Heck, it was expected and described her whole upbringing and struggle to fit in. Standing out among Others, though... She could do without that extra complication in her life, thank you very much.

Iashi considered the cavern's bioluminescent ceiling as they continued to follow Mike. "If there is another reason, I'm not aware of it."

Raven sighed at the honesty in the troll's voice. Raven wouldn't take her frustration out on the troll, nor could she let the ambassador know just how much not knowing bothered her. Instead, the information and experience got filed in the "to be continued" folder. Hopefully, she'd have some time to dig around in Cole's library and find out what this little development meant before it caused any complication to her life.

Argh. Any research would have to wait until after this case and Mike's. They'd already spent way more time chasing Prince Tuguh's trail than she'd intended, and the troll wasn't the only lost child they needed to find.

And then there was Juni.

Raven squeezed her eyes shut. She was no closer to solving that situation than she was before. Juni might be relatively safe for the moment, but staying bound to the Lord of War was unacceptable.

Cole caught up to her and Iashi dropped back to join her troop.

"Feeling better?" she asked.

He scowled at her. He'd needed a moment to collect himself.

"Let me guess." She waggled her brows. "You're going to punish me later."

"You wish."

She waited, batting her eyelashes.

"Okay. You're right." His scowl softened into a grin.

"Music to my ears."

His grin slipped away and he studied her, gaze

smouldering. "You screaming my name is music to my ears."

Hoo boy. She was in so much trouble later.

And she'd enjoy every second.

They walked in silence for a bit. Only the sounds of their footsteps and the pitter-patter of Mike's paws against the cold stone filled the cavern.

Do not be frightened of the unknown, the wild magic whispered.

Okay, that was it. If Raven kept having conversations with the strange power, she needed something to call it. She whispered into the air in front of her. "Do you have a name?"

Cole frowned and peered down at her, a question in his gaze.

A name? What an odd concept. I just am, and always have been.

Raven sighed. She tried. That didn't mean she suddenly accepted having random conversations with magic only she could hear.

Cole leaned over and spoke quietly so the trolls wouldn't overhear. "Who are you talking to?"

She kept her eyes on the fox ahead of her. Mike continued to trot down the corridor, occasionally stopping to sniff the ground and snort in disgust. Trolls didn't smell particularly good to shifters. At least they didn't use any more scent blockers after they entered Torghatten.

"Just asking the wild magic if it has a name," she said.

"Just that, huh?" Cole's lips quirked. "Should I be worried?"

"Healthy competition is a good thing, isn't it?

His gaze danced with mischief before bleeding out to full black. She'd definitely "pay" for this attitude later and her skin already hummed with anticipation.

"No one can compete with me," he finally replied.

"I agree. So stop being silly and suggest a good name for the sentient magic that keeps talking to me."

"Keeps talking to you?" He squeezed his eyes shut for a moment. He tended to do that around her when he needed a moment to collect his thoughts.

"What kind of name are you thinking? Male, female, or something more gender neutral?" he finally asked.

The wild magic chortled and curled around her, flicking her hair. *Call me Vel'am. I always liked that name.*

Cole narrowed his eyes and scanned the area around her. "It definitely likes you. Something must be drawing the magic to your essence."

She nodded. "New perfume."

"Har, har." Cole smiled, but haphazardly. She could practically see the wheels in his marvelous brain turning, calculating, reaching for a logical explanation to make sense of it. His discomfort at not knowing the reason behind Vel'am's actions vibrated through their bond.

The tunnel opened to a large cavern. A number of other tunnels led away from the area, making this some sort of terminus in the underground system of Torghatten.

Their footsteps continued to echo off the rocky walls, but now the sounds of dripping water joined them. Moisture clung to the walls, but the area didn't smell mouldy. A little damp and earthy, but mostly floral and fresh like newly, cut grass, which made no sense. She'd spotted zero flowers or lawns since they entered the tunnels. The only visible organic thing in the dark space was the bioluminescent stuff clinging to the walls.

She veered closer to the side of the tunnel and sniffed.

The lights flared and the smell sharpened. Yup. Definitely the walls. They smelled even better up close. She sniffed again. Were they parasitic or toxic? What would happen if she tried to transplant them?

Cole raised a dark brow. Sometimes she wondered if he stayed with her for the sheer entertainment value, like everything she did amused him. Not in a bad or condescending way, but in a way where he got to relive and experience things in the world again for the first time through her.

"Can we grow these at the Corvid Court?" she asked.

His teeth twinkled with mischief under the glowing in light as he smiled at her. "You want a built-in air freshener?"

The man got her. "Don't you?"

He chuckled.

Mike ran around in a circle and yipped. The hand-over must've happened here. At least she hoped that's what he tried to signal with this spinning act.

She knelt by him. "Do you have the scents of the people the troll was handed off to?"

He bobbed his head.

She reached out and ruffled his white fur.

He pretended to snap at her.

Raven ignored his fake outrage, straightened, and turned to Iashi. "Can we portal out of here?"

The wild magic screeched at her, whipping around her body so fast it scratched her skin. The loud piercing sound rattled her brain long after the magic stopped making it.

Raven winced and held her hand up to no one in particular. "Never mind. I think I have the answer to that."

Before Iashi could question her or her sanity, new footsteps shuffled along the rocky flooring of the cavern.

The group turned in unison toward the new sound.

Instead of darting for cover, Mike placed his fuzzy body in front of her, as if he'd become her fox shield for whatever impending doom walked toward them.

A tall figure stepped into the glow of the cavern from one of the dark off shooting tunnels.

Iashi sucked in her breath and mumbled something in troll to the others. They sheathed their weapons in unison and backed away.

Some escort.

Raven gripped her scythe, the shaft cool to the touch. She hadn't banished the weapon in the tunnels because she'd worried about it counting as using magic. Lugging the scythe through the tunnels hadn't been fun and her muscles already screamed, but now she was glad to have its familiar weight in her hands.

A humanoid figure covered in iridescent scales stood in the light. With reptilian eyes, a flat nose, and a mouth without lips, the entity didn't look like anything she'd seen before.

The stagnant air in the cavern took its time carrying the newcomer's scent to her. She might not have the extremely heightened sense of smell like her fox-shifting half-brother, but her senses were still better than a reg and most other fae.

That thing smelled marvelous.

If Raven closed her eyes and somehow shut off her hearing, she'd envision herself in a spa, floating in a pool of lightly fragranced rose petals and soft, shea butter with hints of vanilla.

Cole cursed.

"What exactly am I looking at?" she asked. More

importantly, could they bring it home with them? She could smell whatever that was all day.

Well, if it wouldn't be a totally weird thing to do.

"A chameleon." The voice of the reptile humanoid scratched against her eardrums. "We're the watchers of Torghatten."

We?

Raven pulled her shoulders back and quickly scanned the area. "Have we done something wrong?"

The chameleon tilted its head. Within a blink of an eye, its body morphed, changing shape and size until Cole's doppelganger stood in front of her.

It even smelled like Cole.

Raven closed her mouth.

The only thing that gave the chameleon away was its eyes. Cole didn't look at her like that, like a blank slate lacking emotion. Oh sure, he probably stared down countless targets with the same dispassionate gaze when he worked as an assassin, but not her. Never her.

The real Cole standing beside her grumbled. "I'm much better looking than that."

The chameleon turned its unsettling gaze to Cole. "But are you?"

The same deep gravel of Cole's voice came out of its mouth, the same voice that had seduced Raven with simple words. The voice that brought comfort in one moment and stirred a deep insatiable need the next.

"Wow," she said. "You're good."

The chameleon dipped its head and transformed back into its natural state. Or at least she assumed that form was its natural state. If the chameleon could transform into anything, then really, anything was possible.

"You've piqued the interest of the wild magic," the chameleon said with its raspy voice. "To answer your earlier question, no. You haven't done anything wrong, and you've paid the price of admission. I merely wished to see why the magic hummed through the tunnels. Now I know."

Well, crap. That sounded ominous as fuck.

She glanced at Cole and he looked just as baffled as she did. No help there.

The trolls still bowed their heads in deference to the chameleon, while confirming they were quite possibly the worst security detail in existence. So, no help there, either.

"My name is Raven Camhanaich. I'm—"

"Branwen Lulu Crawford, Queen of Corvids, daughter of Huginn Muninn, born of Odin, soul-bound to Beul na h-Oidhche gu Camhanaich, Lord of Shadows and patron fae of assassins. Yes. Even we feel the ripples of change in the caverns of the jotun."

Okay...

"It is a pleasure to meet you, bhanrigh. My name is too complicated for the human tongue to pronounce, but you can call me Salril."

"It's a pleasure to meet you, Salril." She bowed her

head. "Did you happen to notice a group of trolls walking this way about four weeks ago carrying a large bag?"

Salril blinked at her, the nictitating membranes closing around his slit eyes sideways. "Yes. They met another group here and handed off the bag before heading that way." He raised a long, skinny, scaled arm to point to a smaller tunnel that led away from where they stood.

"Where does that tunnel lead?" she asked.

"To another part of our domain," Iashi answered.

Oh look, the troll ambassador hadn't lost the ability to talk. Raven would've appreciated Iashi speaking up a little sooner, like when an unknown supernatural creature approached their group from the shadows with unknown intent.

"What was in the bag?" Salril asked.

Raven glanced at Iashi. This wasn't her tale to tell.

The ambassador dipped her chin, silently granting Raven permission.

"Tuguh."

"Tethaahin's child and heir?"

Raven nodded. "He was abducted from his home four weeks ago. We tracked the trolls responsible to this location. We know they handed the prince off here but needed the scent of their accomplices to continue our search."

"And you have it now?" Salril's slit-eyed gaze

briefly snapped to where her brother sat in his fluffy fox form.

"Yes."

"And you're voluntarily helping the trolls recover their lost heir?"

"Yes." Where was he going with this?

"You have no love for the jotun, though from what I hear, your animosity is not unwarranted. Why would you help them now? Is it a love for children?"

"It's a need to protect those who can't protect themselves," she answered truthfully.

Salril blinked again, seemingly accepting her response. At least Raven assumed that's what the rapid blinking meant. The chameleon hadn't attacked her, so that was already a good sign.

"You have a good heart," Salril said. "If you're ever in need, you may enter the tunnels and call upon the magic."

Cole and Iashi sucked in their breaths at the same time. That alone told her the offer wasn't a small thing. Salril's words held significance. If only she knew what that significance was. Obviously, Cole couldn't freeze time and provide an impromptu info session, so she'd have to wait to find out.

If only she could lock herself in the library for another six years and not deal with people or their problems, and somehow continue to keep her family safe.

She dipped her head again. "Thank you for your

generous offer. May I return at a later date to learn more about you and the wild magic?"

The creature's face split open to reveal several rows of sharp pointed teeth. "We would like that very much."

WILD MAGIC SLIPPED FROM RAVEN'S SKIN AS SHE stepped from the tunnel and onto the white slab stones of the Gathering Place.

Again.

Not going to lie, she was getting sick of this place.

Now that Mike had the scents of the new team of abductors, though, hopefully this part of the plan would go smoothly. They needed to tie up this lead quickly so Raven and Mike could turn their attention to Juni's situation or the other missing kid. Surely the police would release the cabin scene soon since as far as Mike's sleuthing went, they hadn't found anything.

The sentinels stepped from their cloaking shadows as they had before. They hadn't changed shifts yet and Raven recognized their faces. She nodded at them and followed Mike as he snuffled along the ground, following the scents of the people who took the troll prince at the hand-off site in Torghatten. With each step away from the tunnel, a growing sense of new dread grew at the base of her skull.

Mike finally stopped in front of the white portal

with glowing flecks of crystalline power. He whined and plopped his fuzzy butt down. He knew exactly whose portal this was, just as she did. They all did, but unlike before, they now knew the unfamiliar scents surrounding the entrance to the portal were from those who colluded with traitorous trolls to abduct Prince Tuguh.

Cole drew up beside Raven, his mouth twisted down. "That isn't good."

"Why not? We know the court the child was taken to. Why are we stopping?" growled Iashi behind them.

Raven turned slightly and waved at the portal Mike sat in front of. "That is a portal to the Realm of Light."

"So?" Iashi spat. "All these portals lead to a domain within the Realm of Light. They took a troll child."

"More specifically, that is the portal to a domain Inari controls." Raven explained. She'd know, she'd visited the place yesterday.

Iashi blinked at her.

"My maternal great-grandmother," she explained to the troll ambassador.

"Do you have reason to believe they're involved? Inari's realm is vast." Iashi paced back and forth. "It could be anyone."

"There are other powerful fae who reside in her domain," Cole added. "Or they could've used Inari's domain as a diversion tactic. Leading us to your great grandmother while disappearing through another portal to travel elsewhere."

"Whether Inari is involved or not, we can't go in there right now," Raven said. "We visited yesterday for an unrelated matter and already stepped on the fae rules for etiquette a little. To go again, so soon, uninvited and demand answers...I'd basically incite a war."

Cole's grim expression confirmed she had evaluated the situation correctly.

Mike chose that moment to transform back to his human form, because a naked ginger was exactly what they all needed right now.

Iashi grumbled and reached into the satchel. She pulled out Mike's boxers by pinching as little of the fabric as possible between her forefinger and thumb and tossed the underwear to him.

The smiley-faced boxers hit Mike in the chest. He grunted, grabbed the underwear and stepped into them, quickly pulling them up. Though being naked was a part of shifter culture and their very nature, but it didn't mean any of them wanted to stand around and discuss intricacies of entering Inari's court with Mike's junk hanging out, Mike most of all. Her brother must've grown impatient waiting for Cole to erect another outhouse weave with his shadows. He didn't speak until his boy bits were covered. "There was something familiar about one of the scents."

"Inari?" Raven held her breath, not wanting to hear the answer. *Please, please, please, don't let it be Inari.*

He shook his head. "No. I would recognize their scent right away."

"But it's familiar? You must've come across it during our trip to their court."

"Maybe. Or maybe they're in the Mortal Realm. Maybe I stood behind them in line for a coffee. I can't place it, so it couldn't be someone who's had a significant interaction with me lately."

She sighed and glanced at the portal. "I can't go in there."

"I can," Mike said. "Let me follow the scent farther and see where it leads."

Cole stiffened.

Raven shook her head. "Absolutely not. The laws that govern me apply to you as well, brother dearest."

He shrugged. "I'll be a white fox with two tails in a domain full of kitsune who shift into foxes with multiple tails. I will blend in. I won't get caught."

"No." She curled her hands into fists. Mike still had nightmares from when he'd been kidnapped by her psychotic ex. Richard had beaten up and chained her baby brother in a seedy basement. Raven had reached Mike in time, but the emotional trauma of those events still haunted him. And even though everyone kept telling her it wasn't her fault. It was totally her fault. "I won't risk it."

"Yet you'll risk a child," Iashi growled.

She turned to face the troll again. "I'm not the one who took him, nor am I the one responsible for his safety. I will do all I can to see the child safe, but I will not risk my brother or a war with Inari unnecessarily. If they wanted him dead, they would've killed him already. This seems like a lot of effort to go to just to murder him somewhere else. We have to assume they have other plans, and we at least know which domain he's in. We'll retreat for now and I'll work on a way to get into Inari's realm without a war so we can find the prince."

"So that's it?" the troll snarled. "You want us to wait and sit on this information?"

The sentinels surrounding them shifted their positions, changing from easy postures to ones ready to draw their weapons and hack Iashi and her troll comrades down at the snap of Raven's fingers. Though their movement was subtle, the troll ambassador in front of Raven narrowed her eyes at the sentinels.

"That's it. For now." Raven spoke softly and placed a hand on Iashi's shoulder.

The ambassador tensed.

"I will do what I can. We'll find a way in." She had other things on her plate already, but she'd help the troll child. She leaned in, placing her face within head-butting distance. "And if I find out this is some sort of elaborate ruse created by trolls to bring me down as some sort of misguided attempt at revenge, my reaction will be swift and brutal."

Iashi gulped and bobbed her head. "There is no

ruse, bhanrigh. We will gladly accept any help you can offer."

That was more like it.

"Now go home and clean house. You have more than one traitor in your midst."

CHAPTER 16

"If I wanted to feel that bad about myself, I'd hop on social media and look at pictures of everyone's perfectly staged lives."

— RAVEN CRAWFORD

Raven rested her head against Cole's bare chest and sighed. This. All the fear and uncertainty of the day disappeared when Cole held her in his arms. He trailed his fingertips along her exposed back, content in their silence.

"Team," Cole said, his breath fanning her hair, his voice jerking her out of her semi-sleep state.

"Huh?"

"Our team of assassins," he said. "Instead of calling them an army. You asked for an alternative."

Had he seriously dwelled on this question for the last two days? And team was the best he could come up with? "Are we trying out for the Olympics?"

Cole sighed. "Squad?"

She laughed. "No."

"You're being difficult."

She drew circles on his smooth skin with her finger. Cole contained immeasurable power, and few matched his strength and skill physically, yet she loved the softness of his patience, his love, his caring, and his consideration just as much, if not more, than the rest of it.

"Since when has that deterred you?" she asked.

He chuckled, his chest rumbling under her head. "Speaking of difficult, you should let me accompany you on the investigation with Mike tomorrow."

Hah. He wasn't even trying to be subtle about his request. "Absolutely not."

"What about Rourke?"

"He's guarding Juni. Besides the last thing I need is Rourke and Mike in the same space. If I wanted to feel that bad about myself, I'd hop on social media and look at pictures of everyone's perfectly staged lives."

"I'll make you feel good," he said. "And I'm excellent backup."

"Should I need any, you'll be the first person I call. But you're not a PI."

Cole grumbled. "You're checking out a cabin, how hard can that be?"

"Careful."

His chest rumbled under her hand. "I'm just saying. It doesn't require any of your specialized PI skills."

"What if we run into someone?" she asked. Had he actually thought this proposal through?

"You'll question them."

"No. You'll scare the crap out of the reg and they'll either crap themselves as they take off without giving us any leads, or they'll dish complete nonsense because they fear their life is in danger from the big bad patron fae of assassins and will say anything to make you go away. This isn't some fae realm or the troll domain. If you throttle or scare them, we get absolutely nothing." Regs were delicate and damaged easily.

"Not true."

She lifted her head to frown at him.

His dark eyes glittered in the moonlight cascading in from the French doors that led to the balcony. "You'll get at least one lawsuit out of it."

She groaned and flopped back into the bed. "I don't know why I put up with you."

"I do." Cole rolled over, pinning her under his body. In one heartbeat, he went from languid and relaxed to predator mode. His dark gaze bled out, making his eyes appear as though made of black onyx.

"I do love your penis," she admitted. And the way he used it.

His grin widened.

"But that's not why I'm with you."

He leaned down and kissed her. They'd been together for six years now—a mere drop in the bucket of Cole's lifetime, but her body still hummed with anticipation when he touched her.

Cole reached out with his shadows to caress her body before he kissed her again. He stole her breath away as he stoked a fire inside of her with his shadows.

Raven didn't have the same natural ability. She "borrowed" the shadow wielding through her anam cara bond with Cole. They'd fused their souls together almost six years ago and became a fae power couple. Juni had tried to give them a celebrity name, but "Coven" never stuck and "Raole" sounded like some sort of pasta dish.

When she told her parents about the bond, they'd been less than impressed. Not because they didn't like Cole, but they felt Raven had acted too hastily in tying her life to the dark fae lord.

If it was a mistake, it was the best Odin-loving mistake she'd ever made.

Cole's shadows continued to explore her body, circling lower and lower as his mouth demanded more than just a taste.

Though Raven already loved Cole when they'd bonded, her need to secure her family's safety and create a proper barrier to protect the mortal realm from Bane's scheming motivated her to make the decision. Cole hadn't tricked or forced her into the life-long bond, despite desperately wanting the anam cara connection with her. And that made her love him even more.

He'd calmly explained the pros and cons, swore an oath not to use it against her and let her make her own decision. Anyone listening to their conversation would've suspected him of trying to talk her out of it.

Cole never hid how much he struggled to let her fight her own battles, not because she was weak, but because he loved her and wanted her safe. He never hid from this truth. He never hid any of his feelings, and let his desires, needs and thoughts flow through their bond.

Right now, he very clearly wanted every cell in her body to sing.

His hands followed his shadows' path, and he tasted her skin, kissing his way down her body, making her ache with need.

First his shadows flicked her skin like liquid heat, then his fingers then his mouth, and then her senses became consumed with him. Only him. He was everywhere. He was everything.

And he had her screaming his name just as he promised.

CHAPTER 17

"I'm going to stand outside, so if anyone asks, I'm outstanding."

— UNKNOWN, PROBABLY
SOMEONE'S DAD

The drive to the remote cabin took hours. The scenery was decent but being crammed in the car with her younger brother and the knowledge Raven would already be at the destination if she flew on her own made her grouchy.

Mike pulled into a little corner store gas station. She leaned over and read the gauge. They'd filled up in the last town, so the tank was almost full.

"We're getting you some food and caffeine," Mike

announced. "I can hear your hangry attitude from here."

She scowled at him.

"You do realize you said that stuff about the decent scenery and being stuck with me out loud, right?"

Oops. "I meant every word. You're not that fun to drive with."

"I'm a fucking saint next to you." Mike gripped the steering wheel, but his words lacked heat. He wasn't putting any effort into being an ass. Instead, he slid the car into the empty parking lot and shoved the gear into park.

Mike turned to her, expression blank. "Any requests?"

"A new brother?"

He rolled his eyes and popped the door open. "Wait here and try not to start an inter-realm war."

Har-de-har-har. So funny.

Her death stare must've instilled a little fear into him because he made a hasty retreat and left her in the car to jog into the questionable corner store. The last time she'd let him grab snacks from a gas station like this, he'd purchased meat pies and they both spent the next twenty-four hours fighting over who got to throw up in the toilet.

Meat pies.

Canada had never been known for its meat pies. Mike had been talking to a lot of Kiwis from school at the time and thought it would be a great idea to give meat pies a try after hearing so much about them. The only problem? He got them from a random convenience store in the middle of nowhere.

Her stomach turned and a wave of light-headedness flowed through her.

Ugh.

Mike opened the car door and slid into his seat. Without a word, he dumped a bag of chips on her lap and placed a coffee in the holder between them. "Enough cream to make it beige."

She smiled and held up the bag so she could read the label. "Sour cream and onion?"

Mike shut the door and pulled the seatbelt across his chest to click it in place. "Would you have preferred ketchup or dill pickle?

She blanched. Those flavours might be Canadian classics, but she'd never liked them. "I guess I should be thankful you didn't opt for meat pies. You're not trying to kill me, yet."

Mike shuddered and slid the gear into reverse. He navigated out of the parking lot and got them back on the road.

"Those pies were awful," he admitted. "One day, I'll go to New Zealand and taste the real thing."

"Please do."

He narrowed his eyes at her.

She smiled sweetly and opened the bag of chips, offering them to Mike first. He shook his head and she proceeded to stuff the food into her mouth. Maybe she had been a little hungry.

About half an hour later, Mike turned the vehicle onto a dirt road. According to the phone's GPS, they'd reach the cabin in five minutes. The large evergreen trees shrouded the road in shadows, but occasionally streams of sunshine broke through and danced across the windshield. This cabin really was in the middle of nowhere.

The bumpy road jostled the vehicle and Raven's stomach rumbled. The chips had tasted like chalk and a dusty film coated her mouth. She shifted in her seat and used the controls to put her window down a few inches. Maybe the fresh air would help settle her stomach.

"Are you okay?" Mike glanced at her.

"Perfect. Why?" She stretched her neck to get her face closer to the outside air as it funneled into the vehicle.

"You've gone really pale."

And she's started to sweat. Why was it suddenly so hot in here? Her stomach clenched. "Pull over."

Mike didn't bother questioning her. He slammed on the breaks and stopped the car in the middle of the rural road.

Raven clicked free from her seatbelt, threw the door open and flung herself from the vehicle. With a few steps, she made it into the wooded area of the forest and emptied her stomach behind a salal bush.

Again.

This wasn't like her.

"You're beginning to make a habit of this." Mike called out from the car.

"And I'm beginning to think you really are trying to get rid of me." She followed the wide trail farther, ignoring Mike as he called out to her. He couldn't complain if he couldn't see or hear her.

Dry moss and pine needles covered the path. Indents in the dirt indicated this area had once been used as a road of some sorts. Maybe for dirt biking.

Her gut twisted and she staggered to the nearby bush to hurl again.

"That's it," she muttered to no one else. "No more gas station food. Ever."

"Really?" Mike spoke somewhere behind her. "That's what you're going to blame this on?"

She started to straighten from her hunched over position when her attention snagged on fresh tire imprints. She waved Mike over.

"Nuh-uh. We're not that close, Rayray."

Seriously? He'd held her hair when she puked into some random vase at the entrance to Inari's court. Seemed like an odd time to try to set boundaries. "Fresh tracks, you nitwit."

Mike squinted at her as if to visually assess if she lied before taking a few cautious steps toward her. He pulled his shirt over his nose as a makeshift mask.

Such a baby.

She grabbed his arm and hauled him forward, taking extra steps to distance them from the puke bush.

"They're up here, too." She pointed at the impressions in the soil. "And here."

"And thankfully all upwind," Mike muttered.

She opened her mouth to say something because clearly, she couldn't let her baby brother keep poking fun at her.

He held out a stick of gum.

Mother trucker. She snatched the peace offering from his hand, ripped off the wrapper and chucked the gum into her mouth.

Peppermint. *Mmmm.*

While she stuffed the wrapper in her pocket, she used her aggressive chewing to convey her displeasure.

Mike snorted and walked farther along the path, sniffing the air as he went.

"Anything?"

"Just forest and gasoline. Whatever drove in either drove out or stayed put. No individual scents."

"Isn't this trail heading toward the cabin?"

Mike nodded and held up his phone, so she had a view of the map displayed on the screen.

The birds chirped in the trees and the heavy smell of sweet pine in the air helped soothe Raven's nausea. The mint gum helped a lot, too, but she'd never admit that to Mike. Yeah, she was in her thirties now, but that didn't mean she couldn't be petty.

After a few minutes passed, the roiling in her gut

eased away, leaving her feeling as she had before. Yup. Bad chips. She'd never trust Mike with his food choices again. *Fool me once, shame on you. Fool me twice...*

Mike stopped and sniffed the air again. His brow furrowed.

She looked ahead on the path. Metal glinted under the sun.

Oooo shiny.

"Is that what I think it is?" Mike asked.

"A bumper," she said.

They continued forward and the closer they got, the easier it became to make out the shape of a vehicle under leaves, branches, and ferns.

"A burgundy SUV," she mused.

Mike held up his phone and waved the map back and forth. "The cabin is just over five-hundred metres away."

She grabbed a branch and pulled it from the vehicle's roof.

"Definitely burgundy," Mike agreed.

"Any scents?" As a raven shifter, she benefited from heightened senses, but Mike's sense of smell didn't just rival her abilities, it eclipsed them.

Mike shook his head. "A suspicious absence of smells. Started a few feet back."

"A blocker?" Witch charms could do almost anything nowadays, especially if someone had the funds to back their wishes. The witches sure had been busy lately. She'd never encountered so many scent-blockers being used in such a short span of time.

"Most likely," Mike said.

She shrugged and continued pulling off the debris from the vehicle. The stronger the witch, the larger the radius the scent blocker covered. Whomever made this charm had been powerful. "More than one way to identify the most recent occupants."

Instead of replying, Mike shoved his phone in his pocket and helped remove the branches. After a couple minutes of work, he tried the door handle. "Locked."

Pffft. Like that would stop her.

"Licence plate removed as well. Think they filed down the VIN?" Mike asked.

Raven pulled her lock set from her pocket and winked. "Let's find out."

Her twin taught her how to pick locks years ago and the skill had come in handy more than a few times —professionally and personally. The skill hadn't taken long to *pick* up, shattering all her previous beliefs in home security.

Raven inserted the tension wrench into the bottom part of the keyhole first. Keeping the tension wrench in place with gentle pressure, she inserted the pick into the top of the lock next. She raked the pick back and forth, pushing down on the pins each time she pulled back with the pick. In less than a minute, she set all the pins. The lock popped and when she swung the door open, stale air hit her face.

"Nothing," Mike growled. "Magic is such a bitch sometimes."

"Well, we're learning that the mom went to a lot of trouble to hide her tracks. None of your background checks turned up supernatural abilities."

"My *thorough and comprehensive* background checks," Mike corrected.

"Yes, yes. You're the best."

He straightened and puffed out his chest.

"You're also ridiculous." She pulled a twig from her hair and tossed it to the side.

His smile widened.

"Felicia Johnson is a reg," Raven continued. "Either she paid someone for the charms with money she saved or she had someone else helping her."

Mike rubbed his hands together. "Bank time."

She narrowed her eyes at her baby brother. "It's like you're looking for an opportunity to break the law. Don't glare at me like that. You already look like Bear, there's no need to start acting like him, too."

Mike scowled but turned his attention to the driver's door, or more specifically the door jam. The sticker with the vehicle's information, including the VIN had been seared off, leaving charred remains of the sticker.

Raven leaned over the hood and looked through the windshield. Gashes marred the otherwise smooth dashboard where the VIN should've been.

"Looks like someone took a knife to it," Mike spoke

behind her. He ducked inside, leaned across the middle console and opened the glove box. "No registration papers."

"Pop the hood."

Mike settled into the driver's seat sideways with his feet still planted on the ground outside the vehicle. "Why?"

"Something Marcus taught me."

Bear's best friend, Marcus, the same witch who routinely supplied her family with charms and wards, also happened to be a damn good mechanic. He often said being a witch was what he was, being a mechanic was what he loved.

Used to her shenanigans, Mike didn't argue and popped the hood.

She lifted the hood and locked the stand in place. The smell of engine oil tickled her nose. Leaning in, she located the firewall and smiled. There, glaring and obvious, stamped to the firewall, was the VIN.

Mike climbed out of the SUV and walked over, his feet crunching dried leaves and snapping the branches they'd removed from the vehicle. He stopped beside her, leaned in and whistled.

"Is that what I think it is?" he asked.

"Not many people know the VIN is also stamped or etched on the firewall or other key components of the engine like the transmission, as a security measure against car theft and chop shops," she explained.

Not sure how much of a deterrent that posed to

actual car thieves, but at moments like this, Raven appreciated the extra effort.

Mike pulled out his phone and snapped a picture of the VIN. His fingers flew across the screen, most likely accessing his main computer remotely to run the information. He'd have a name for them soon enough.

"Let's check out the cabin." Raven straightened and surveyed the forest. "Walk back to the car or shift and go from here?"

"I'll take the ground." Mike tugged off his shirt and chucked it on a nearby bush. "Turn around."

Having no wish to see her brother's junk, she did as he asked and watched the wind play with the leaves and sway the treetops.

Little teeth nipped the back of her leg.

"Odin's sac." She hissed and spun around, ready to swat at her brother, but he had already dashed out of kicking range.

With a playful yip, Mike ran through the brush in his fox form, his fluffy, white body disappearing in the forest.

Argh. She didn't get to call him cute to his little, fox face.

She stripped and folded her outfit into a neat stack beside Mike's discarded pile of clothes. Sure, she'd mastered shifting her clothes to a void while in her conspiracy form, but it took a lot of energy to perform the task and she found it drained her during flights. Since she had time, she'd undress.

A gentle breeze moved through the forest, carrying fresh scents of pine and cedar. She closed her eyes for a moment and enjoyed the rustle of the tree branches overhead and the calm serenity that came from being outdoors and away from the bustle of the city.

When she finally called the corvid essence, the energy infused into every cell of her body rose up and splintered her into a large conspiracy of ravens. The birds took flight and her consciousness directed them toward the cabin. Some of the birds spotted a streak of fluffy, white fur dashing along the ground beneath them.

While directing a couple birds to keep watch, she paid little attention to Mike's progress and aimed the rest of the birds toward the small, square building nestled in a copse of evergreens. No sounds came from the cabin, no smoke from the fireplace. A fire wasn't needed at this time of the year during the day, but usually the scent of wood smoke clung to the air from nighttime use.

The birds perched on the roof and hopped along the eavestroughs. Some took to the tree branches and surrounded the building, essentially creating a three-hundred-and-sixty-degree view of the cabin. She pinged from each bird, taking in their vantage point to catalogue information from the outside of the cabin.

Back when Bear behaved like a nincompoop, her conspiracy had dwindled in numbers. Neither of them had understood their powers strengthened when they maintained close proximity. She'd scoffed at Bane when he told her Bear was her soulmate. She'd grown irritated and confused when Cole confirmed the information. And now she accepted that while both involved a close, unbreakable bond, fae soulmates were not the same as the ones she read about in paranormal romance books. Her bond with her twin had nothing sexual to it, so Bane didn't deserve a punch in the face for telling her Bear's role in her life. He deserved tons of violence for a myriad of other unrelated things, but not that.

Bonding Juni as his guardian sat at the top of the list.

Asshole.

A genius asshole, but still an asshole.

The conspiracy shifted and croaked, unsettled by the wave of negative energy rippling through them from her wandering thoughts.

Mike shot from the underbrush and without hesitation raced to the doorway. Keeping his nose low, he sniffed and huffed, circling the entrance.

She sent a bird down to check for open doors or windows in case she missed anything from her panoramic view. Nothing.

The police had already searched the cabin, so it wasn't imperative that they get in. At least not right away. If they couldn't find a trail to follow from here, though, they'd revisit the cabin.

Mike sprinted around the cabin, occasionally skidding to a stop to sniff and snort an area. He reached the back of the building and his fluffy ears perked up, pinging forward. Mom was right, he really was adorable. She just wanted to pick him up and snuggle, even though he was her brother.

One of her ravens croaked and the sound echoed through the forest.

Mike turned and bobbed his little, fox face. He'd found their scents.

Raven launched the conspiracy. A few would stay with her brother to keep tabs on him and his position, and the rest would fan out and look for the missing boy and his mom.

Hopefully, the mom took supplies with them and had another safe place to hole up in. Despite the summer weather, the Canadian forest wasn't a place for the average person to hang out for an extended period of time. They'd entered bear and wolf territory and the majority of the campgrounds in this area required hard-side campers to stay.

The birds played in the airflows, the gentle summer bands of warmth provided a playful romp and a nice distraction from thinking about outcomes. After ten minutes or so, Raven reached a slow-moving river. Nestled behind the riverbank and a large rock face sat another log cabin—so small it probably qualified as a shack. No road led to the building, and it was located well past the standard five-hundred-meter search area from the original cabin. Even if the police had searched on foot, they wouldn't have detected the presence of this building.

A woman in her thirties sat on a large boulder near the riverbank. She looked like an extremely haggard version of Felicia Johnson's driver's licence. She wore black sweats, a hoodie and sneakers, and the sad defeated look on her expression cut at Raven's heart.

A boy fitting the description of Kayden Smith sprawled on a blanket with a tablet near the woman. He wore the standard summer outfit of loose-fitting shorts and a baggy T-shirt. And even with the headphones on, the sound of whatever game he played on the tablet trickled to her birds.

Gotcha.

Instead of waiting for Mike, she embraced her corvid essence and forged a path to the clearing where she'd folded her clothes. Felicia needed to be confronted and that meant Raven needed clothes. She dressed in under five minutes and transported back to the shack.

The boy didn't notice her arrival and continued to play on his tablet.

Felicia squeaked and sprawled back. Losing her balance on the rock, she fell to the mossy riverbank.

Raven stood still and waited for the woman to collect herself. When Felicia finally stood, her gaze widened before scanning the forest behind Raven.

That's right, I'm alone.

"How...Who..." Felicia Johnson stammered before clamping her mouth shut.

"My name is Raven and I work for Crawford Investigations."

"And you came alone?" The woman reached for the long, hunting knife strapped to her belt. "Isn't that risky?"

Raven pulled on her powers and the scythe of Corvids popped into existence and snapped into her outreached hand.

"Please don't do that." Raven nodded at the woman's weapon.

Felicia blanched and dropped her hand.

Mike ran into the clearing and skidded to a stop. Panting, he stood ready, muscles tense, weight shifted forward.

"A white fox! Cute!" The boy threw off his headphones and scrambled to his feet.

"Kayden!"

His mom's shrill scream froze the boy where he stood. Slowly, he turned to face his mom and Raven. His eyes widened and his mouth dropped open.

Raven sighed. Why was she always made out to be the bad guy?

The tension in Felicia's body didn't ease away, but her expression changed. Instead of angry and hostile, it morphed to determination. She stepped away from Raven and gathered her son in her arms. She held him close and met Raven's gaze over his head. "Please don't take my son."

The boy stiffened in her arms before gripping her tightly and hugging her back.

"That's not up to me," Raven said.

Felicia's grip on Kayden tightened. "You can't take him. He can't go back. It's not safe."

Raven rocked back on her heels and glanced at Mike.

He continued to pant and offered no guidance whatsoever.

"Why do you believe it's not safe?" Raven asked. "How is he in danger?"

"That vile ex-husband of mine wants to use him."

Use him? "As what?"

The woman took a deep breath but kept her son in her arms. "He wants to use Kayden as an anchor to the Realm of Light."

Well, that escalated quickly.

CHAPTER 18

"My life feels like a test I didn't study for."

— RAVEN, EVERY ODIN-LOVING
DAY

R aven didn't have a chance to question Felicia and her bold claim. Three light fae warriors snapping into existence a few feet away prevented that. Not bothering with introductions, Raven lifted her scythe and pulled on the power of the Shadow Realm.

Mike backed up into the bushes. She loved her brother, but a fox shifter had no special defence against three fae warriors, especially without a weapon. Maybe his unlocked divinity would give him the edge in the future, but knowing Mike, he hadn't taken much time to find out what simmered beneath his fur.

Mike made the smart decision and removed himself from the equation—if they got their hands on him... If they knew what that snarky ginger-haired computer geek in the form of a fox meant to her...She'd rend the realities of this world and the next to save him.

Maybe they should make a grab for him to motivate her ass-kicking skills.

No. That would be bad, Raven. Bad.

"We have no quarrel with you," one of the fae said. Golden hair billowed around his chiseled face in soft waves and his golden armour reflected the sunlight, threatening to blind her.

"What do a bunch of light fae want with a reg?" Okay, Felicia literally just gave her a giant clue, but that information only explained why the father wanted Kayden. Did these rollers want the boy for the same thing? Or did they want to eliminate Kayden to foil Christian Smith's plan? And why would they come after Kayden, specifically, when a whole realm of reg children ran around? What made this child different? Special?

"That's none of your business," a second fae said.

Raven refrained from eye-rolling, but it was really hard. She might be an adult, but that didn't exclude her from having angsty adolescent moments.

Instead of cowing to the three warriors, she stepped in front of the boy and his mom and pulled more of the shadows to her. The magic thrummed in her veins. Her heart pulsed in time.

"Look lady," the third warrior addressed her now. "I don't know who you are or which dark fae underling is your daddy, but this isn't a fight you can win."

They didn't recognize the scythe.

To be fair, scythes were a popular accessory in the Underworld. Hers wasn't the only one with skulls on the blade, either. Sure, her jeans and T-shirt might be the opposite of intimidating, but the corvid and shadow energy she wielded should've tipped them off.

They couldn't sense her power. She didn't bother to hide her smirk as the reason for that struck her. They couldn't be very powerful if they missed her energy signature. "I'd appreciate it if you didn't try to deflect your daddy issues on me."

Fae number three snarled.

Nailed it.

"Who sent you?" she asked. "We all know you're not important enough or powerful enough to think up this little abduction plot on your own." She twirled her pointer finger in the air at them. The fae might be swordsmen, but Raven's abilities negated the threat of a physical violence in most instances.

"What makes you say that?" Number Two frowned.

"You don't know who I am."

They exchanged glances. The first and second fae had enough intelligence to look concerned, where the third warrior just looked like he wanted to smash something—probably her face.

The possibility of ending this amicably never really existed. Not when these three were obviously pawns on someone else's game board. Why did they bother entertaining a conversation with her? Just that inexperienced? Unsettled by her presence and unsure of how to proceed? Or were they stalling for someone else? Something else. Something nefarious.

Raven scanned the forest, keeping the bulk of her power surrounding her, Felicia, and Kayden, like a magical force field of sorts. She sent shadows shooting out in thin tendrils to the forest. Lots of life—trees, bushes, shrubs, mice, deer, brother...no other regs or fae.

The first warrior paled. "Shadows..."

Raven grinned. *That's right, boys. Shadows.*

Where wielding a scythe was hardly unique, wielding shadows was entirely different. Only a few fae could manipulate shadows as she just did—number one being her husband Cole. His mastery still left her in awe, and not just because he used them to do naughty things to her.

If Cole had been standing here beside her, these three fae would've already been killed for the threat they posed to her life. Cole didn't pause. He never hesitated. He was quick, lethal and efficient.

Raven didn't think or operate like Cole. She wanted information.

The first fae warrior had already begun to connect the dots of who stood in front of them. He must know or at least suspect his group's chances of surviving a physical altercation with her were low. Yet, he hadn't tried to leave. None of them had. Instead, the three fae looked at each other and clenched their jaws. Steely determination took over their expressions, while the sun continued to glint off their armour without any emblems to identify their master.

"Who sent you?" She resisted the urge to twirl the scythe in her hand. Rourke had caught her off-guard in their sparring matches a number of times. He said showing off and gloating were moves for dead morons.

Her guardian wouldn't know sugar-coating if he got trapped in a candy store.

Raven kept her muscles loose and her stance easy. Shifting her weight more to her toes, she waited. Their initial attack would give her an idea of what tactic they'd use and what defence she should apply. Juni wasn't the only Crawford who'd spent these relatively calm years training.

If they were smart, they'd coordinate in a unified attack. If they were idiots, they'd strike one by one.

The fae fanned out in front of her, unsheathing swords and calling trickles of radiant energy to them.

Their power barely registered to her senses, so that wouldn't be an issue. The sharp edges of their blades could still cut her, though, and underestimating them could be fatal. She internalized her magic, letting the power radiating from the scythe consume her.

As the fae lunged at her in unison, she became a flurry of motion, the scythe an extension of her body and power. Step, lunge, tumble, turn, swipe, spin, slash, duck, sweep, cut, dodge, strike.

Raven lost herself in the motion, in the dance of death. Juni had once called it the samba of slaughter as a joke, but her sister wasn't wrong. Raven fused with the scythe, adopting the single focus of destroying the enemy until they no longer posed a threat.

When her consciousness withdrew from the scythe's power, she stood in the middle of the clearing. The bodies of the three light fae lay strewn on the grass around her. Within a few more seconds, she regained all her senses.

The wind continued to rustle the leaves and the burble of the river flowing by brought a tranquility to the environment that didn't match the blood pooling at her feet or her heartbeat thudding in her ears.

She didn't sense any injuries on her person. When she merged with the scythe this intensely, the adrenaline-like magic sometimes masked the damage she sustained during the fight. If the light fae landed any strikes, they couldn't have been that bad or she'd feel the sting or ache by now.

Raven turned to find Felicia clutching her son, holding him tightly against her body. "Ready to go?"

Felicia's lips trembled. "Who are you?"

"I'm Raven Crawford and if you want to live, you'll do as I say."

CHAPTER 19

"I'm on a seafood diet. I see food and I eat it."

— UNKNOWN, BUT ALSO RAVEN

After transporting Mike in fox form to their clothes, Raven used the shadow portals to take Felicia and her son to the Crawford's family home. Contractually, she should deliver the boy to his father. Legally, she should take both of them to the police to return the boy to the father and have the mother arrested, but morally... Morally, she couldn't hand over an eight-year-old boy if his safety was in question, even in the slightest.

Mike had to drive the vehicle back from the cabin, which meant he wouldn't return home for hours. Mom and Dad were out. So was Juni and she hadn't responded to any of Raven's texts. Weird. That girl was permanently attached to her phone. If Bane was involved with her silence, Raven would find some way to hurt him.

Setting Felicia and Kayden up in the kitchen that looked out to the backyard, Raven served them bologna sandwiches and water.

The boy quickly whipped out his tablet, shoved his headphones on and went back to ignoring them, as if getting transported through a shadow portal by the Queen of Corvids was no big deal. In his defence, he had no idea who she was and neither did his mom.

It took Mike less than a minute to figure out how the light fae had found the mother and son. Although the cabin had a remote location, the tablet had managed to connect to the internet when Kayden and his mom went to sit by the river. It took Mike another half a minute to disable the feature on the tablet so the light fae hunting Kayden couldn't use the same trick twice.

Felicia scanned the room, taking in every detail and visibly trying to piece together what was going on. From her pinched brow, she still hadn't put all the pieces together. Felicia had the same thick wavy hair as her son, so black it looked like waves of midnight. She'd be striking under normal circumstances. Her piercing green eyes looked haunted, yet the creases around her mouth said she smiled a lot. Or at least used to. Things had changed.

Right now, Felicia studied her son, a small sad smile tugging at her lips. "They grow up so fast, you know?"

"No, actually." Babies and kids and additional responsibilities might be in Raven's future, but not right now. The demands of her position were intense. She had to ensure she lived long enough to have children first.

"Oh, well." The other woman tore her gaze away from her son and turned her attention to Raven. "Maybe one day you'll understand what I mean."

Raven shrugged. Her plans of procreating weren't any of this woman's business. "Why do you feel your ex-husband is going to use your son as an anchor to the Realm of Light?"

"You wouldn't understand."

Seriously? Raven had just transported Felicia and her son via shadows and the woman questioned her ability to understand supernatural stuff? "Since I'm currently trying to decide what to do with you and your son, why don't you go ahead and tell me anyway."

Felicia sighed, long and drawn out, like taking the time to explain the situation to the woman who decided their fate was painfully inconvenient. Maybe Raven should've transported them to the dungeons at the Corvid Court, instead. That would've sped things up.

And also prove Cole's theory on fear tactics.

Thankfully, Felicia started talking. "A dark fae queen erected a barrier between the Realms almost six years ago."

You don't say.

"The barrier still allows movement, but it's more restricted and the queen's sentinels monitor travel and enforce restrictions," Felicia continued.

"That isn't anything new," Raven pointed out, opting not to reveal her role in the very events Felicia now described.

"Well, there's a faction of roller groupies called the Lighters. They're mostly harmless regs, but there are a few shifters, witches and other Mortal Realm supernaturals in the group."

Raven nodded and waited for her to continue. Roller groupies weren't a new thing. Juni had come into contact with some a few weeks ago for a case, but this was the first time Raven heard the term Lighters. How were they different from any of the other roller worshipping plebes?

"They've been trying to find a way to anchor their souls to the Realm of Light so they can travel there when they die."

Raven's brain stuttered. Apparently, people needed to find new ways to be dumb. "The Realm of Light isn't heaven. Even if they succeed with this anchoring, they won't find rebirth in a utopian society.

They will indenture their souls to the light fae instead."

Felicia placed her hand on her chest. "I know it's stupid. My ex doesn't."

"How does your son figure into this?"

"They believe a sacrifice will tether a pathway in place for their souls."

Raven's stomach twisted. Nausea bubbled up.

Oh no, you don't, stomach. Don't even think about it.

Raven swallowed and continued. "Why would your ex-husband volunteer Kayden? Does his own son's life mean so little to him? Or is he that fanatical?"

Felicia dropped her hand from her chest and laced her fingers together. "He knows Kayden isn't his biological child."

CHAPTER 20

"The brain is the most outstanding organ. It works 24/7, 365 days a year from birth until you fall in love."

— SOPHIE MONROE

Questions bombarded Raven's mind: Who's the father? Is that what made Kayden different from other reg children? How'd Mr. Smith find out? Why was he granted full custody of a child who wasn't his? She opened her mouth to start asking the torrent of questions when the front door opened.

Raven closed her mouth and paused to listen. Her sister's scent flowed down the hallway.

Juni slammed the door shut and growled before stomping down the hall. She walked into the kitchen, took in the guests and froze.

"Everything okay?" Raven asked.

"Nothing is okay!" Juni blurted out, gaze wide, eyebrows raised. Without another word, she spun on her heel and stomped to her room in the basement.

Raven turned to Felicia and considered her options. She couldn't leave the mother unattended. They still hadn't figured out who the vehicle was registered to. Felicia gave all the indicators of being a reg, which meant she was either resourceful or she had help. If Raven left her unattended, she might try to run or contact someone. Raven could deal with those things, but she'd rather not place her family and their home in unnecessary danger.

But she also couldn't ignore the hurt and confusion on Juni's expression.

Without an explanation, Raven flicked out a knife and sliced her finger open.

Felicia jumped back in her chair.

That's right. I'm dangerous.

"Bjorn Crawford, I summon you." Raven repeated the summons two more times for good measure in case her twin tried to ignore her.

Felicia's eyes widened.

At first nothing happened. Raven stood in the room as Felicia narrowed her eyes more and more until they were just slits, barely showing the green of her eyes.

Then the air stirred. Magic whipped around Raven and vibrated along her skin. The shadows in the room drew together more and more until a doorway made of swirling bands of shadow writhed a few feet away from Raven.

A large man stepped through the portal. Wearing a leather jacket over a plain shirt, ripped jeans and an annoyed expression, her twin scowled as the portal snapped shut behind him.

"A blood summoning?" Bear ran his hand through his thick black hair. "Really?"

"You weren't answering your phone," she said.

He glowered and pulled out his phone. He glanced at the screen and his eyes widened.

"I'll appropriately grovel and explain this later." She waved her finger between Felicia who appeared shell-shocked and her son Kayden, who still hadn't looked up from his tablet or noticed a man walking through shadows. "I need you to watch these two. Don't let them out of your sight. No phones. No computers. I already deleted the messaging apps on the tablet."

"Why?" Bear folded his arms across his chest.

"Because I asked nicely?"

"You need a refresher course on manners if you think that was nice." He fake sighed and pleaded with the ceiling theatrically. "She was such a down to earth person before she became the queen."

"Queen?" Felicia wheezed.

Great. Not only did she have to put up with Bear's attitude, but he just gave up that information.

"Just watch them," she said.

"Fine. Then you can explain what all these missed calls and voicemails are about," Bear said.

She was going to murder her own soulmate. "You could use this time to actually listen to them."

When Bear had fallen hard for Cole's twin sister, Chloe, they'd all hoped she'd be a positive influence in Bear's life. She was, but a lot of Bear's asshole-like tendencies still flared up, just proving the love of a good woman alone didn't change a man. Luckily, Chloe loved and accepted Raven's brother just as he was.

Instead of throttling Bear, Raven left the dining room and followed her sister's steps to the basement. She had a lot of fond memories of her old bedroom, all featuring Cole.

Mmmm.

She reached the bottom of the stairs and knocked.

"It's me," she said though she wasn't sure why. With Juni's superior sense of smell, her fox-shifting sister already knew who stood on the other side of the door.

Juni didn't respond. No permission granted to enter, but no screeching for her to go away either. Raven cautiously opened the door and stepped into Juni's large basement bedroom.

In the centre of the room, her sister moved

through a series of complicated postures and strikes. Faster and faster, Juni spun around the room with twin daggers in a vicious combination of maneuvers. A fae kata—one of the more advanced ones from the look of it.

"I expected to find you crying into a pillow." Raven leaned against the door jam.

"Do you know me at all?" Juni finished the kata and straightened from a bow. "What do you want?"

"I want to know what's up with you and whether I can do anything to help." And more specifically, who did Raven need to hurt?

"What's up with me?" Juni snarled. "What's up with you?"

Oh, wow. Juni must be really unsettled to resort to this kind of response. Nothing unsettled Juni. Nothing except... "Does this have anything to do with Lincoln?"

Juni tensed and then her shoulders drooped as if all her energy just drained out of her. She stood that way for a long minute, the mental battle playing out in her head evident in her pinched expression. "I don't know what to do about it."

"About Lincoln?"

"No. It." She waved her daggers in the air as if to demonstrate what "it" was.

"You're not making any sense." Raven walked around her vibrating sister. "Why don't you put the knives down so we can talk about *it* without me risking a stab wound?"

Juni squeezed the grips of the daggers and stared at the ceiling.

Raven had that effect on her siblings.

Instead of pushing Juni farther, Raven took a seat in one of the two leather armchairs in the room.

Juni grumbled, slapped the daggers down on the dresser and flopped into the other chair. The old leather creaked. "I've never done it."

Raven forced her face to remain neutral. Juni was twenty-one now. She'd gone on plenty of dates, but they never developed into relationships, at least not any long-lasting ones. Relationships weren't necessarily required for having sex, though. Bear had certainly proven that enough times during his single days. Raven always figured her sister took after Bear and adopted the "love them and leave them" mantra.

"Do you want to do it?" Raven asked, softly. Some people didn't and that was okay, too. If anyone pressured her sister into something she didn't want to do, well...

"Yes," Juni whispered.

"With Lincoln?"

Juni nodded.

Raven tried not to shift in her seat or show any reaction on her face. Though she loved her sister and considered them close, they'd never talked about sex.

"So what's the problem?" Raven asked.

From the way Lincoln looked at her sister like she

was his favourite dessert, Raven doubted the feelings weren't reciprocated.

"What if I suck at it?"

Raven bit her lip. "I'm pretty sure Lincoln would enjoy that."

Juni snarled and leapt from the chair. She began to pace back and forth. "I'm serious, Rayray. What if... what if I'm bad at it? I've never met anyone I've wanted to go there with before and now I feel like I'm going into battle unprepared."

"Did you run off on Lincoln?" Poor guy.

Juni winced and nodded.

"The first thing you need to do is talk to him. Communicate."

Juni cringed.

"I know. It's not my specialty either. But Lincoln should know, and I think discussing your feelings with him might put you at ease, and it will also help him understand why you ran off." Lincoln was probably naked and confused somewhere. And hurt. Men had feelings, too.

"What if he doesn't want me?" Juni asked.

"He does."

"But what if?"

"Then he's a moron and not worth your time."

Juni nodded more to herself than Raven. At least Juni had stopped pacing. Her younger sister was always confident, always sure. Seeing her like this unsettled Raven and made her heart ache.

Raven shifted forward in her seat and leaned toward Juni. "Sex isn't like some kata, Juni. There are no pre-set movements or requirements. Talk to Lincoln and then have fun."

"Have fun?"

"Yes. Have fun. It's meant to be enjoyable. Finding out what you like and what your partner likes is half the thrill. Tormenting them with that knowledge is the other half."

Juni's face screwed up. "Odin's shriveled nuggets, you're actually making sense."

"I do that sometimes."

"Can we forget this conversation ever happened?"

"Not a chance."

Juni groaned and flopped back into the worn leather armchair. Her phone buzzed in her pocket. When she slid the device from her jeans and read the screen, she paled.

Raven took that as her cue to leave. She stood and walked to the door. Before she left, she turned to her baby sister. "Remember, just talk to him. Preferably in person."

Juni gulped and nodded. She placed the phone face-down on the coffee table. "Who are the strangers upstairs?"

Hah! Juni didn't even try to segue to a new topic. "Kayden Smith and his mother, Felicia Johnson."

Juni perked up, still ignoring her phone. "You closed the case?"

"Yes. Sort of."

Juni didn't respond right away. If Raven listened closely, she might hear the wheels in her sister's head clanking around.

"Why do you look like you sucked on a lemon?" she asked Juni.

"The mom looks familiar. I was trying to place her face. Bane has a picture in his cabin of a similar looking woman."

"How similar? Same woman, just in different clothes or with a different expression similar? Or sister similar? Distant relation?"

Juni shrugged. "I don't know. I've been blocking memories of that creepy place."

"Did you see the plaques?" Bane had questionable taste when it came to interior decorating.

"Of course, I saw those fucking plaques." Juni took a deep breath to visibly relax. "Do you think he hung them himself or got some poor servant from the Realm of War to do it?"

"I don't know. I got through my time there by imagining a big, badass, dark fae warrior whose only dream growing up was to serve the mighty lord, but after he worked hard to rise through the ranks, he discovered he landed an interior decorating gig to the most neurotic sociopath in existence."

Juni laughed. Her gaze lightened and the shadows that had clung to her features eased away. "Poor dark fae underling."

Juni's phone began vibrating again.

"I'll leave you to it." Raven turned her back on whatever rude hand gesture her sister waved at her and walked to the door. She reached for the handle and the tell-tale tingle of Underworld magic whipped through the room.

She spun around.

Bane stepped from a portal, wails of tormented souls and a red haze announcing his entrance. "Time to go, my little Vixen."

Juni curled her hands into fists and straightened her back. "Right now?"

"I'm headed to court. You must attend me." He held out his hand, looking like a gentleman, when they all knew he was quite the opposite.

"What in the Underworld, Bane." Raven folded her arms across her chest. She had no recourse for stopping Bane from taking her sister. He had all the cards in his hands, and it grated against her last nerve. "You've survived how long without a caomhnóir? Surely, you're not so weak as to need her now."

Bane's gaze brightened and he waggled his finger at her. "Trying to shame me into leaving your sister here? Tsk tsk, Raven, dearest. You wound me. And here I thought we were basically family."

"Family doesn't torment one another."

Bane lifted a dark eyebrow. "Have you seen your family interact?"

Crap. He had a point there. "Not seriously torment each other."

He smirked.

"You don't need Juni." She waved her hand at her sister, who spent the time quietly collecting her daggers and strapping them to her legs.

"You're right." His grin widened to the point she could count how many of his teeth she'd like to knock out. "But I want her, and she's mine now. You're in no position to barter."

Raven gathered her power. She couldn't kill Bane, but maybe if she hurt him a little, he'd rethink his decision to try to insert himself into the Crawford family.

"It's okay, Rayray," Juni muttered. "I'll go."

Raven tried to say something but only a snarl came out.

"He can't force me to stay with him at all times. I'll be back." Juni stepped toward the Lord of War and slapped her hand into his.

Bane's gaze gleamed with unspoken emotion and he winked at Raven before pulling her sister with him to the Underworld.

Raven clenched her hands, threw her head back and screamed at the ceiling, releasing the magic she'd built up to throw at Bane. The house shook with the power.

She stood and seethed, her mind running through all her options and not liking a single damn one.

"Are you okay?" Bear yelled down the stairs.

No. Nothing was okay. Nothing was all right. She turned to the door and called up before her twin decided to come down and check on her. "I'm fine."

Bear didn't yell anything back to her, so he'd obviously accepted Raven's response. Instead of leaving right away, she pulled out her phone and texted Lincoln: *Satan has her. She'll call when she escapes his evil clutches.*

Poor guy was probably still waiting for Juni to respond to his messages. Her sister didn't have the chance to text him before she left with Bane and cell phones didn't work in the Underworld.

I hate him, Lincoln texted back.

So did Raven, yet Juni as Bane's guardian was strangely not her biggest worry at the moment. Though it was difficult to admit and accept, Juni could take care of herself. Raven had to let go of the idea she could control everything in her siblings' lives.

She'd still search for a way to free Juni, but right now, she had to help two different abducted minors, one of whom sat in the dining room upstairs.

CHAPTER 21

"Always late, but worth the wait."

— BEAR CRAWFORD'S PERSONAL
MANTRA

R aven utilized every single one of her manipulation techniques to keep Bear from storming over to the Underworld to find Juni and rip her a new one after she quietly updated him on recent events in the corner of the kitchen. She kept her attention on Felicia and Kayden, but neither had made an attempt to flee or make contact with anyone else.

"Fine, then." Bear settled down. "I'll just have to kill Lincoln."

"Do you even hear yourself?"

He scowled.

She purposefully left out that her initial reaction had been the same. "You don't get to kill Lincoln. Juni loves him and if you murder him, you'd make her sacrifice worth nothing and then neither of your sisters would ever speak to you again."

"Not exactly punishment," he interjected.

She scowled at him and continued. "You also don't get to behave all protective when you're days late to the outrage party. Maybe if you'd answered your phone or responded to the voicemails, you'd get to act all put out, but you missed out on that opportunity."

He threw his hands up. "I was in the Underworld."

Odin's twinkle berries. "Why would you go there?"

"To meet Erebus." His flat voice gave away his feelings on meeting his father-in-law. Their father-in-law. Chloe and Cole were twins after all.

Meeting one of the primordial gods, the God of Night specifically, had intimidated Raven. Erebus commanded the power of darkness and his presence felt like raw energy grating her skin. But meeting Cole's father paled in comparison to meeting Cole's deranged stepmother, Nyx. That maniacal goddess had low-key kidnapped Cole and tried to kill him. When Raven and Rourke sprung him from her clutches, she'd merely shrugged and walked off, while Erebus promised to have a word with her.

Ugh.

"Went well?" she asked.

"About as good as you're guessing. I pretended to be outraged by your summons, but it was really the best thing to happen to me."

"I take back my rant."

He grunted, which perfectly demonstrated the extent of his communication skills.

Raven's phone dinged and she pulled it from her pocket to read the text message.

Car registered to Joseph Beauchamp, Mike had written. He must've taken a break from driving and checked his search remotely.

Raven glanced up to find Felicia watching them from the dining table. She'd already had two glasses of water, a coffee and a visit to the powder room. If Raven didn't figure out what to do with the current situation soon, she might have to start serving something harder.

And here Raven thought her days of serving people were over.

"Does the name Joseph Beauchamp mean anything to you?"

The woman paled. "He's a friend. He helped us out."

"A friend who knows enough to park five hundred meters away from the cabin and hide a vehicle from aerial surveillance? A friend who knows how to remove almost all of a vehicle's identification numbers to avoid detection? A friend who used a scent blocker and disappeared without a trace and no detectable method of transportation?"

Felicia gulped.

"That's some friend," Bear remarked.

"Who is he?" Raven pressed. What she really meant to ask was: *What is he?*

"A friend."

"He's mommy's special friend," Kayden said as he tapped his tablet screen.

Raven raised her eyebrows at Felicia. The woman's cheeks darkened by several shades of pink. "We don't like to use labels."

Bear chuckled and shook his head. That must've hit close to home.

Raven leaned over and whispered to her twin, "It sounded just as lame when you used to say shit like that."

"I can hear you," Felicia said.

Raven straightened and ignored her brother's glare. "I'm sorry. That was unprofessional of me. My brother brings out the worst in me."

Felicia harrumphed and crossed her arms.

"What can you tell me about Joseph?"

Felicia frowned. "I'm not going to provide any information that will get him in trouble."

Raven sighed. "I'm not the police but fine. Let's investigate how your ex planned to sacrifice your son. How did you find out? How much do you know of the process?

How did your ex discover your son's true lineage and who is Kayden's biological father? Is he in the picture? Does he know Kayden's his? Do I need to worry about any supernatural beings barging through my family's front door? I don't feel like killing any more people in front of your son."

Felicia paled and looked away, wrapping her hands around the tall glass in front of her. She stared at the empty contents. "That's a lot of questions."

"Let's start with one at a time."

She nodded. "I discovered the plot because I still have access to Christian's emails. That lazy oaf never bothered to change the password." She held both her hands up. "I know. I know. It's a serious breach of privacy, but he's acted so weird lately and hasn't provided satisfying answers to my questions about Kayden. I'll do anything for my son, including hacking into Christian's email."

"What did the email say?" Bear asked.

"I can forward it to you. I sent it to myself," she said. "And I deleted it from the sent folder, just in case."

Smart. "Please send it to me, but in the meantime, just paraphrase as best you can."

Felicia nodded again. "He said he had an eight year old to offer for the sacrifice. Someone else questioned him and he replied that the boy wasn't even his. I don't know how he found out."

"And the groupies were okay with this?" Bear

asked. "The life of an eight-year-old reg isn't as valuable as their guaranteed path to the Realm of Light?"

Felicia pressed her lips together. "Disgusting. Isn't it?"

"Guess it explains why they're motivated to secure a way to what they think is heaven. They're definitely not good enough to get there on their own," Raven said. Even if Kayden weren't Christian Smith's biological son, he'd still probably spent years raising him as his own. How could he turn off love like that?

"Makes it worse knowing the Realm of Light is far from what they're actually looking for," Bear added.

"How did your ex get full custody?" Raven's stomach twisted again. Those nasty chips. *Thanks, Mike.*

"He's a lawyer and the primary earner," Felicia said. "And I used to be an addict."

Hmm. That meant the ex-husband could make things difficult if they confirmed Felicia's claims and tried to fight the law for her. Raven pondered the situation. The ex must've discovered Kayden's parentage after he used his lawyer tricks to push for full custody. Driven by what must've been intense anger and bitterness, he somehow decided to take his emotions out on Kayden and offered the child he'd raised as his own for eight years to the Lighters as the sacrifice. Complete conjecture, but what else made sense?

Raven continued to fill in the blanks. Christian Smith started acting shady as fuck and Felicia, picking up on his change in behaviour, used his login credentials to read his email and discovered his heinous crime. Or at least, his plan to commit a heinous crime. With the help of an unknown friend, she took her boy and ran. Everything made sense yet didn't at the same time. Raven still had so many questions. Why would an intelligent lawyer be stupid enough to discuss the possible murder of his ward in emails? Who was the friend and why did this roller group have a complete disregard for life? And why did they think a child's death would grant them the access they craved?

Hopefully, Raven would get answers to the first question once Mike returned with the vehicle and flexed his computer skills. The forwarded email from Felicia might help, but Mike didn't need it. He was that good.

As for the mystery man, Raven had a theory. She tapped her phone's screen and scrolled through her photos until she found the one she wanted.

She held up the picture to Felicia. "Is this Joseph?"

The woman flinched, giving away the answer before she spoke. "Yes."

Raven rotated her wrist so Bear could view the screen. They'd captured this picture from the security cameras set up around their house when the dark fae lord had visited Juni a few weeks ago.

"Let the record state the witness has identified Bane, the dark fae Lord of War, as the person behind the alias Joseph Beauchamp," Bear said.

"Oh god!" Felicia's gaze wildly searched the room, flicking to every corner of the room before she slapped her hands over her face. Her whole body trembled. Her hands muffled a loud sob and she rocked back and forth. She made a low keening sound that made the hair on Raven's arms stand up.

What could Raven say to that? How could she console the woman having a nervous breakdown in front of her? At least Bane's identity explained the unknown friend's special skills at police evasion.

Felicia took a number of deep breaths before managing to peel her hands from her face. Without meeting Raven's gaze, she whispered into the table's polished surface. "I didn't know."

Bear turned to Raven. "Bane obviously believes the Lighters' hypothesis has merit. He wouldn't want someone else to forge a path through the barriers because they'd have an advantage instead of him."

"So he helped Felicia escape with the boy to thwart their plans," Raven finished the theory. "But that doesn't fit Bane."

Felicia stopped crying and her gaze snapped between Raven and her brother, her brows pinching in.

Bear nodded. "He doesn't help unless it serves a bigger purpose. He could've just killed the kid."

"Or used him to make his own pathway." Raven tapped the kitchen counter. "He didn't suddenly grow a conscience."

They turned in unison to the boy still madly

playing a game on his tablet, oblivious to their discussion and his mom's concerned expression. His black hair shone under the bright dining room's light, and his smooth face and defined features hinted at the handsome man he'd become.

The truth hit Raven like a sledgehammer. "Bane's the father."

CHAPTER 22

"It's like no one appreciates that I stay up all night overthinking for them."

— RAVEN CRAWFORD

Raven padded from the master bedroom of her Corvid Court and stepped onto the large stone balcony. The wind curled around her, a little too cold to be refreshing, but scented with deep florals and an exotic magical tang Raven had grown to love. She still couldn't accurately describe what the air in the Shadow Realm smelled like, but if pressed, she'd say glittering pixie dust.

Raven walked to the stone railing, closed her eyes and inhaled. She leaned the scythe against the stones and rested both hands on the cold surface. She had all these pieces to a giant puzzle, and she still hadn't figured out how to make them all fit together. Surely, she could use the information about Bane's son somehow to get him to release her sister from her bond.

But could she use a child?

The breeze continued to roll past her, flicking her hair in every direction. The moon cascaded silver and red light onto the stones and lit the long drop to the ocean below.

Two enormous ravens emerged from the dark abyss of the night sky and perched on another section of the railing about ten feet away from her.

"Hello, Father," she said.

At least twice the size of regular ravens, the black birds launched from the railing in unison. With heavy beats of their wings, they hovered in the air like a dark omen from some sort of thriller movie, their sleek black feathers gleaming under the silvery bands of moonlight. They swooped down, careening into each other with a loud croak.

The air shimmered and in place of two birds, a large, intimidating man stood in their place. Dressed in black fae armour, his dark Other gaze swept the balcony as he slowly closed the distance between them with the grace of a vicious warrior. A long, flowing cloak made of raven feathers trailed behind him and slipped along the stone surface with each step. Huginn Muninn, her biological father, stopped in front of

Raven and peered down at her, dark brows furrowed, black gaze blazing. "Daughter."

She smiled and leaned forward to give him a hug. He stiffened and awkwardly patted her back before she released him and moved away to a more acceptable distance. As ravens, Huginn and Muninn, thought and memory, were known to all of the Underworld as Odin's spies and greatest creation. The Allfather forged the birds from his own essence and protected the blood of his blood fiercely. Huginn Muninn wasn't supposed to have the ability to father any children. But he'd met Mom, fell in love, and did exactly that. Odin had been furious when he found out and threatened to kill Mom if she ever entered the Underworld. In a self-less move, Huginn Muninn left Mom to keep her safe and remove her from Odin's radar.

And he still loved Mom, though he'd never act on it now.

Despite growing closer to Huginn Muninn over the years and having respect for him and the sacrifices he made to ensure her well-being and that of her twin brother, he'd never replace the man who raised her as his own—Terry Crawford—and to the man's credit, he didn't try to.

"I take it this isn't a social visit," she said, noting his furrowed brow hadn't eased since he took his human form.

"Bane has bound your sister to him as a guardian," he said, his deep voice echoing into the night.

Her stomach twisted.

"Yeah. Old news. What concerns me is how you know."

"He dragged her into his audience with Odin and introduced Juni to the entire court as his new caomhnóir and the Corvid Queen's much loved baby sister."

Raven swore.

"Now all your mutual enemies have a new shiny target. Taking out the Lord of War's guardian and the Queen of Corvid's sister is like taking out two ravens with one arrow."

"Two birds with one stone."

He waved his hand in the air. "Whatever. It amounts to the same thing. You're all in more danger."

Crap. She'd been wrong to assume Juni's relative safety in Bane's presence. Really, who'd try to take on the Lord of War? "Wait a minute. Our mutual enemies?"

Huginn Muninn nodded, his frown deepening.

"There are people who've lumped me and Bane into the same category?" She shivered. The audacity.

"That's what you're concerned about?" He tilted his head. "Mortals are so confusing."

"I'm not exactly a Mortal, now am I? But no." She sighed. "I just...can't...with all of this right now."

"Why don't you tell me what happened. Give me something to go back to Odin with that would explain why Juni would make such an ill-advised move as to bond herself to your sworn enemy."

So she did. She ran through the events, cringing with each sentence. She stopped at the point Bane took Juni to court. Though she trusted Huginn Muninn, he was still his father's creation. Still his spy. He couldn't act against Odin if ordered, and Raven didn't want the information about Bane's son to get out. At least not until she decided what to do with Kayden.

"Elizabeth is divine now?" he whispered. His gaze flicked to the sky as if he contemplated flying away with his next breath. Flying away to Mom.

Oh no.

That wouldn't do.

While Mom, Juni and Mike had the blood of Inari running through their veins that gave them longer lifespans in addition to light fae powers, Dad didn't.

Realization hit her in the face like a sheet of ice. She staggered back a step. Growing up as a half-fae bastard, she'd known her entire life, she and her twin would most likely outlive the rest of their family. Raven had come to terms with that about as well as an ostrich with its head in the sand adjusted to the weather.

But now...

Now it wasn't just her and Bear with extended lifespans. It was everyone *but* Dad. That just seemed so wrong. So unfair. So...lonely.

Why had it taken her so long to realize that? Did the others know? Had they figured it out, too? Had Dad?

They'd all have to watch Dad get old and...She shook her head. No.

She didn't like this line of thinking at all. Her stomach dropped and air escaped her lungs.

Huginn Muninn watched her, his mouth turning down, his gaze softening. "We all have to say goodbye at some time. It never gets easy."

"Don't you dare get any ideas," she snapped. Did he plan to wait out Dad before courting Mom? Her stomach twisted again.

Huginn Muninn recoiled. "Your mother chose a good man, a man who raised you when I could not. A man who loved you when merely acknowledging your existence would get me or you and your brother killed. I would never dream of interfering in your mom's relationship with a man I admire and respect." His gaze drifted away again.

He might not harm Dad. He might appreciate Dad and honour Mom's choice, but the longing pinching his expression spoke of lingering feelings and the glimmer in his gaze hinted at long term plans being made.

Oh no.

CHAPTER 23

"No more battle bra."

— RAVEN CRAWFORD, FOR THE
BAJILLIONTH TIME

Raven waited in her courtroom for her guest to arrive. Cole and Rourke stood behind her, giving her the silent support and confidence she needed. She could do this. If she played her cards right, she'd get what she wanted and help Kayden.

A red portal of smoke formed in the center of the court. Along with waves of heat, the smell of charred bones radiated from the swirling doorway to the Realm of War. Bane stepped from the bloody red haze wearing full court armour and a scowl. Before the portal snapped shut, two more figures stepped out of the portal.

Juni stood behind Bane wearing fae armour as well. Even her baby sister got to fully cover herself with metal.

That's it. She was commissioning new armour. No more battle bra.

Lincoln stood beside Juni and held her hand. He looked just as deadly as he'd become, swathed in the same black matte armour Cole preferred.

Both Juni and Lincoln looked to have recently showered and her sister practically glowed. When Juni exchanged a look with Lincoln, the heat carried through the room.

They must've had time to sort things out.

Despite the seriousness of this meeting, Raven smiled. Good for them. Juni deserved to be happy. All her siblings did.

Bane followed her gaze and glanced behind him. His deepening scowl said exactly how much he approved of this new development.

Hah! Even better. Rock on, sister.

"I hope you haven't wasted my time summoning me here. There is only one offer I will accept." Bane's deep voice echoed against the black stone walls.

Crows, ravens, and magpies lined the parapets and observed the meeting with beady eyes while the

Shadow Realm's red moons bathed them with ethereal light.

Coming from Raincouver, Raven had worried about holding court without a roof, but Cole explained the spell providing a weather shield over the building. If it did rain, she could activate the spell and keep everyone dry.

Or drown her guest like the rat he was.

She liked having options.

"Are you sure about that?" Raven asked. Hopefully, Bane would change his mind about only accepting one deal. She had something he wanted more. Or at least she thought she did.

Bane narrowed his eyes.

"What if I have a better offer?"

Bane rested his hand on the hilt of the sword strapped to his waist. "I'll humour you by listening. Tell me about this deal and why I shouldn't try to kill you where you sit while I use your sister as a shield."

If Raven didn't have her own insurance policy, Bane's words would've chilled her to the bone. Even now, ice clung to her spine and threatened to freeze her in place.

"Well, out with it." Bane tapped his foot. All attitude, no fear. He knew they wouldn't kill him because they'd do anything to protect Juni. Capturing him was an option, but a difficult one to execute, and given the opportunity, he might hurt or kill Juni to spite them. They couldn't risk it and he knew it.

"You will release Juni from her bond," she stated.

"This is getting tiresome." Bane crossed his arms in front of his chest. "But I'll play. Why would I do that?"

"You'll do that because it will be a fair exchange."

He frowned. His dark eyebrows almost forming a V. "For what?"

"You mean for whom." She let her smile widen, feeling the pieces of this puzzle fall into place and possible victory. "For your son."

Instead of anger or resignation, Bane reacted in the most unexpected way. He laughed. And laughed. And laughed.

She sat back in her throne of iron feathers, frowning and drumming her fingers on the cold metal armrest, while Bane laughed his fucking head off.

Cole and Rourke shrugged in unison when she looked back at them and Juni looked confused.

Bane's laughter finally subsided into chuckles. "Oh, Rayray. You continue to find ways to surprise me."

She frowned harder. She hadn't expected this reaction at all. She'd expected anger. Maybe even some cursing, not humour.

"Do you know why I like ravens?" Bane asked.

Raven drummed her fingers along the armrest again. She'd lost control of this meeting and she didn't like that. "No, but I'm guessing you're going to tell me."

"They're resourceful," he replied. "They're survivors."

"Will you agree to the deal or not?" she asked.

"No."

"No?"

"I said what I said."

"I have your son and your lover held captive. I could return your son to Christian Smith and let him use your son's life and the dark fae magic running in his veins to puncture a hole through the barrier and establish a path to the Realm of Light. A path you will not have access to. A path that will undermine whatever twisted plans you have for the Mortal Realm."

"You won't do that." Bane shook his head, still chuckling.

"Why not?"

"You're too soft to sacrifice an innocent boy. You won't give him to that sorry excuse of a human, and you certainly won't hurt or harm him yourself. For these sorts of deals to work, I have to believe you'll actually go through with your threats," he said.

Bane certainly had her number. "You seem confident I won't stoop that low to protect my sister. Who's also innocent, by the way."

"Not the way these two have been at it, she's not." Bane smirked and jerked his thumb at Juni.

Her sister and Lincoln turned almost the exact same shade of red. If Raven weren't attempting to orchestrate her sister's freedom, she'd laugh at the turn in conversation.

"You won't do it," Bane repeated. "Even if you

tried, your entire family would stop you. Morals can be so pesky like that."

"Free my sister and I'll free your son," she said.

"Saying it in a slightly different way won't change the results," Bane said.

Cole had said something similar to her when she'd spoken with the sentinels. She needed a different tactic. "I might not have it in me to kill your son, but I'm not above keeping him from you."

Bane's hand curled into a fist.

Got you.

"It's a fair deal," she said.

"I'm giving up my caomhnóir who's your sister. You're only giving up my son. He has no special value to you nor a special place in your life."

She waited, knowing he needed to barter. It was all a part of the fae dance. How long ago did Kayden go missing? Why did Christian choose Crawford Investigations to search for his missing child? Did Bane somehow manage to manipulate Christian to use Crawford Investigations? If so, why had Bane put so much effort into hiding Felicia and Kayden if he wanted them to find his son? To protect them from the others who searched for them? Why not take his son to the Domain of War with him instead? While Bane might have confidence in their PI skills to find his child where others failed, he'd taken a huge risk, if in fact he'd planned any of this.

The more she thought about it, though, the more

she felt like a pawn on Bane's chessboard. Had Bane orchestrated everything to reach this point? And why? What was his end game?

Bane straightened and speared her with a look. "I will release your sister from the caomhnóir bond and return her to you, alive and unharmed. In exchange, you will return my son to me, alive and unharmed and assist me in destroying the Lighters group."

She hesitated. The wording gave her a lot of wiggle room by not specifying how she helped him. She could work with that. She could work around that. Why would a dark fae lord give her such an easy deal to agree to?

She frowned harder. And why would the Lord of War want or need assistance with a group of roller worshippers? Wasn't this what he lived for? Didn't he thrive on war and bloodshed?

Bane nodded as if he followed her entire mental processing. "It's a good deal, Raven. Agree to it."

"I will, but...why?" Why had he gone easy on her after all this time and effort? Why relent now?

"I need your help," he said.

CHAPTER 24

"A woman should be three things—intelligent, strong and badass."

— R.H. SIN

I *need your help.* Bane's words caused Raven's brain to misfire. "Can you repeat that?"

The Lord of War scowled.

Guess she pushed it a little too far. Pulling on her power, she blended realities to reach into her inventory and withdraw a short rope. About an inch in diameter and three feet long, the fae rope radiated power. Though the material wasn't crucial, only the intent, Raven wasn't taking any chances with this deal. Not when her sister's freedom was on the line. "Let's finalize the agreement."

"With a fae rope binding? Really?" Bane sighed.

"I insist."

"Fine." Bane reached out and wrapped his chaotic death magic around the rope and spoke in fae. She still hadn't become fluent in the language—the dark fae made the most complicated sounds with the simplest vowels and simple sounds with a string of consonants. It had taken years for her to wrap her brain around the Irish-like language, but she could at least follow Bane's words.

He said something along the lines of, "I, Bane, Lord of War, hereby swear to release Juniper Crawford from her caomhnóir bond and deliver her alive and unharmed to her home after Branwen Lulu Crawford, Queen of Corvids has returned my son to me, alive and unharmed and has helped me defeat the Lighters."

Raven shook her head. "We release and return our loved ones now. If anything happens to either of us, I don't want my sister dead and your son in limbo."

"How do I know you won't use this as an opportunity to stab me in the back?" Bane asked.

Raven sighed, the thought had crossed her mind. The deal said nothing about keeping Bane safe. "We'll add it to the agreement." She wrapped her magic around the rope and wrenched it from Bane's control.

"I, Branwen Lulu Crawford, Queen of Corvids, Daughter of Huginn Muninn, swear to release Bane's son alive and unharmed immediately following this agreement in exchange for Bane releasing Juniper Crawford from her Caomhnóir bond. Once Juni and Kayden's safety and freedom are secured, I will assist Bane in defeating the Lighters. I will not act against Bane nor seek him harm, and he will not act against me nor seek me harm until our business with the Lighters is concluded and we have returned to our respective homes." She peered at Bane. "Is that satisfactory?"

He nodded. After she coated the rope in her power, he repeated her actions, making his pledge in fae again.

The entire time, a small tug teased the corner of his mouth as if he'd finally tricked her. She went over the promise in her head and couldn't see it.

Dread tingled her spine, but she mentally shrugged the feeling away. She'd get Juni back. Her baby sister would be free of cumbersome fae lords, and Raven could figure out the new problems caused from this deal later.

Bane's magic enclosed around her own and the rope. The power of their promise folded the material until it pulled tight in a knot.

Done.

Bane turned to Juni and held her face in both his hands.

She stiffened but held still instead of punching him. Her expression told everyone in the room how much she disliked Bane's touch.

Lincoln vibrated, looking ready to launch himself at the Lord of War, even though it wouldn't do any good.

"Oh, Juni," Bane crooned. "Our time was short and sweet."

Ugh. Gag me.

"When your lover has lived his measly reg life and his body is a dried husk, come find me. We could have some fun, you and I." Bane smiled.

Juni's defiant expression fell, and the colour drained from her face.

Lincoln stood stoically at Juni's side. He flinched at Bane's words, but he didn't have the same blindsided look Juni had. He'd already figured out what Juni's released divinity meant in the long run.

And he loved her anyway.

Raven definitely couldn't kill him now. She just wanted to hug him.

Energy snapped through the room. Bane must've broken the caomhnóir bond because he released Juni's face and stepped back. He turned away from her as if she were one of those "save the world" people running a survey downtown who just wanted a moment of his time. The slight grimace in his expression was the only giveaway that something unpleasant had occurred and most onlookers would mistake it for disgust.

Juni staggered and shook her head. The broken bond, must've packed quite the punch, because Juni sucked in a deep breath and squeezed her eyes shut.

Raven had no idea what a broken guardian bond felt like, but the look on Juni's face told her it wasn't pleasant.

Juni visibly collected herself and turned to Lincoln, lips trembling. He opened his arms and without hesitation, she stepped into them, her legs buckling at the last second. Lincoln caught her and held her tight. Over Juni's wild red hair, Lincoln's gaze locked on Raven's, with an unspoken question.

She nodded. Those two did not need to be here for the rest of the meeting.

With one arm wrapped possessively around Juni's waist, Lincoln used the other to throw down a lodestone. A portal snapped into place and Lincoln pulled Juni through the swirling depths to her room in the Mortal Realm.

Once the portal snapped shut, Bane turned to Raven and brushed his hands together as if he'd actually gotten them dirty. "Bring me my son."

"You really are an asshole," she said. "You know that, right?"

His widening grin answered for him.

CHAPTER 25

"Alone time is the best time."

— RAVEN CRAWFORD

F inally alone with Cole in their bedroom after a long day, Raven flopped down on the bed beside her anam cara wearing only a tank top and undies. The bond connecting them vibrated with warmth. Cole preferred her to sleep naked, but this was the next best thing.

"Are you sure we should stay here? Maybe we should check on Juni," she said.

"We sent Rourke and he said everything was fine. Our assassins are watching over your family, and we know Bane doesn't currently pose a threat to them.

They're going to be okay." He sat down on the edge of the mattress and reached over to rub her back. "At least physically."

"I can't get over the look of devastation on Juni's face." Raven spoke into her pillow, her mind travelling back to the moment Juni realized she'd live hundreds of human lifetimes and Lincoln would only live one.

Somehow Cole understood the reference. "An extended lifespan can be more of a curse than a blessing."

"She finally found someone to love and now she's facing the reality she'll have to live without him."

Cole continued to rub her back. "She will still have a lifetime with him if everything works out. That's all she would've had if she hadn't unlocked her divinity."

"It's not the same."

"I know."

His sad tone made her look up. "How many lovers did you have to say goodbye to?"

"Too many to count." His gaze twinkled. He was messing with her now. "Thousands."

If she weren't so comfortable sinking into the mattress, surrounded by the fluffy duvet, she'd smack him. "Answer the question."

Cole sighed. "I have never had to say goodbye to a lover the way you're referring. I never met anyone worth that kind of exquisite pain." He smiled and drew swirly lines down her back. "Not until now."

"Ah, but we will have many lifetimes together.

You'll probably grow bored with me in a hundred years."

"And trade you in for a younger model?"

She snorted.

He leaned down and kissed her neck. "Never."

His mouth moved along the sensitive skin, turning up the heat on this relaxed moment and stirring a familiar need inside her.

Mmmm. Yes. She loved his mouth. He did wonderful, magical things with his mouth. She knew what he was doing. Cole often distracted her from over analyzing situations to prevent her brain from burning out.

Raven wanted nothing more than to melt into the building desire and answer the needy ache, but her mind still tried to process and reflect on today's events.

"Why do you think Bane was so happy with the deal?"

Cole sighed and rested his forehead against her back. "Why wouldn't he be happy? He got his way."

"But so did I," she said. "That doesn't fit with the Bane I know and hate."

Cole rolled onto his back to lay beside her. "You're right. He was uncharacteristically happy, but I kept going through the wording of your fae oath and couldn't find any faults. I would've spoken up if I had. If anything, Bane was too vague, too broad on his requirement for your help. He didn't specify how you had to assist him. He also specified destruction of the group, not any individual person, so you have a lot of room to maneuver when it comes to interpretation."

"My assessment as well."

"Yet, both of us saw that smirk," Cole said.

"We're missing something," she said.

"We'll deal with whatever warped plan Bane conjures up." Cole turned his head to the side so his dark gaze locked on hers. He reached out and held her hand by his side. "Together."

She smiled and closed her eyes, enjoying the normalcy of this moment, of Cole's tenderness. He might be lethal personified, but in moments like this, he was just a man comforting the woman he loved.

"Together," she agreed, squeezing his hand. "Now come back over here and you can finish showing me how much you appreciate this original prototype."

A wide smile split Cole's face and his teeth flashed in the diminishing light. "My pleasure."

He took less than five minutes to remove her tank top and underwear, but he somehow made it feel like hours of exquisite torture in the best way possible. He'd had years to learn her body and every spot that needed an extra flick of the tongue, brush of shadow or added pressure. He'd mastered her body, wringing out her pleasure until she shook and moaned in ecstasy.

Tonight was no different, yet just as special. Her body ached for him, and his devilish shadows and wicked tongue had her hanging on a precipice, ready to fall over the edge. He settled between her legs and pushed inside with a single, deep thrust. She tilted her hips up and met him. They both moaned.

Yes, this. Cole was all she needed in this life and the next.

"You're everything to me," he whispered in her ear before kissing her neck.

Prepared to launch into how much she loved him, she lost her words. Right when she planned to speak, Cole began to move and shattered her world all over again.

CHAPTER 26

"Nobody likes Bane."

— MIKE, STATING THE OBVIOUS

Raven flopped down on Mike's super-sized beanbag and grabbed the tennis ball from its makeshift perch. In worn jeans and a basic T-shirt, she enjoyed the Mortal Realm attire as a nice comfortable reprieve. Leaning back, she threw the ball against the wall and caught the rebound.

She never understood this activity. Was it supposed to help her relax? Focus? Improve her reflexes?

It didn't seem to do any of those things, but it did give her something better to do while she sorted through her thoughts and waited for Mike. The alternative was eating and though deep-thinking-eating was up there with stress-eating and boredom-eating, her stomach hadn't recuperated from Mike's latest attempt to kill her via food poisoning.

Oblivious to the death stare she aimed at him, Mike sat at his desk seemingly studying multiple screens at once while his fingers flew across the keyboard.

"Have you heard from Juni?" he asked without looking up.

"No." She went back to throwing the ball against the wall. "How long do we give her before we send in an extraction team?"

"At least a full day." Mike paused to drink some coffee before resuming his techie stuff. "I'm sure Lincoln will smooth things over. They're probably busy with other stuff."

"Ew."

"Yeah." He picked his mug up again and drank some more. Had he slept at all last night?

"What are your thoughts on the Smith case?" she asked.

"We're definitely not handing the kid over to that sicko."

Like Bane would let them do that anyway. "I think that goes without saying."

"So, it's whether we want to go to the police before or after we help Bane defeat the Lighters," Mike said.

"I think the police should come after. We don't want to tip off Christian."

"I thought that as well." He pushed away from the computer.

"You're thinking of how to bill him?"

He nodded and typed while he spoke. "If I wait, we might never see financial compensation for the time and resources we put into this job."

But it wasn't about the money, not really. He'd take a financial hit over risking a child any day of the week. They all would. "But if you bill before, you either have to bill without closing the case, which will hurt your pride and the business reputation, or you close the case, which will involve disclosure of Kayden's current whereabouts and tip off Christian anyway."

"Exactly."

She caught the ball and held it to her chest. "There must be some way we can bring this all together. Close the case, receive payment and set a trap to destroy the Lighters in one strike." The thought had already crossed her mind, but there was one problem with the idea.

"I'm not comfortable using the kid as bait." Mike's fingers flew across the keyboard. *Tappity-tap-tap.*

She sighed and the tension in her neck muscles eased away. "Me neither."

Mike stopped typing and he furrowed his brows. "So we need to think of a way to keep the kid out of it and keep you safe."

She frowned. That was an odd thing for Mike to say. "We need to keep everyone safe."

"Except Bane," Mike added. "Nobody likes Bane."

"Truer words have never been spoken. I'm going to meet with Bane next and formulate a plan. I'll try to work in your billing. It may be the ticket we need to get in the door."

"You have an idea," Mike said, mischief dancing in his gaze.

"I do." And now she needed to pull it off. "I need to find out more about the Lighters first."

RAVEN SPREAD THE PRINTOUTS OF CHRISTIAN Smith's emails across the dining room table. She could look at them on her phone, but sometimes it helped to print them and lay them out to view all at once. It helped establish patterns without having to flick between different windows. And maybe she was just old school, and her eyes needed a break from the screen.

The front door opened and closed. No slamming, which thankfully meant no drama. Usually.

Juni walked into the kitchen. Instead of a curt hello before retreating down the stairs to her basement room, she nodded at Raven and took the seat beside her.

"Are you okay?" Raven asked.

"Of course. Why wouldn't I be?"

"You just realized you have an extended lifespan and Lincoln doesn't. I had my whole life to come to terms with this possibility if I dated a reg. You didn't. So I'll ask again. Are you okay?"

Juni sighed and picked up one of the papers. "Yeah, I guess. We just got together but the idea of outliving him hadn't crossed my mind. The information blindsided me."

"Lincoln wasn't blindsided," Raven said. "He already figured it out."

"How do you know?" Juni placed the paper down and picked up the next one.

"He looked resigned, if anything. He'd already realized he'd grow old and shriveled while you continued on as the goddess you are."

She dropped her head.

"And it changed nothing for him."

"I know." She continued to study the evidence, but her mouth curved into a gentle smile. "What am I looking at?"

"Email correspondence between Kayden's father and his faction of Lighters. He's a lawyer, so he's careful with his wording, but if you read between the lines—"

"He's a heartless bastard," Juni filled in the blank.

"Worse."

Juni frowned at the paper in her hands and held it closer.

"If you're going to give me a hard time about

printing them, you don't need to bother. I already know I'm old." Raven squashed the urge to gather up the papers and hide them from her sister. She had to own this.

"No, it's not that." She cut her gaze sideways. "Though you totally are."

Raven growled.

Her baby sister ignored her and picked up another paper and held it beside the first one. "It can't be her."

"What?"

She placed the papers down to pull out her phone from the pocket of her pants. She tapped and scrolled the screen and gave away the precise moment she found what she sought. Her lips jerked into a smug smile.

"Remember me telling you about that case I had with the burnt house?" Juni asked.

"Yeah, it's the case where you met Hikaru." If that light fae weren't already dead, she'd slaughter him or stick him in a jail cell beside Frey for the rest of his measly existence.

"He was sent by Inari to watch over the roller group."

"I wondered if there was a connection, but there are so many different branches within the Lighters, and we haven't had time to search for one." Until now.

"You don't need to." She tapped her finger on the paper resting on the dining room table. "This is Mrs. Baker's email address."

"Sunshine69?"

"Her favourite thing and her firstborn's birth year, apparently."

Raven snorted. "Do you know why Inari wanted Eveline's roller group watched? Why this group in particular?"

Juni nodded while still scanning the papers. "Apparently, they sought a way to tether their souls to the Realm of Light."

Raven squeezed her eyes shut for a second and tried not to crinkle the printout in her hand. "Why are you just now telling me this?"

"Well, if you haven't noticed, there's been a lot of other things going on." Juni placed the page back on the table and turned to her. "And I didn't think it was relevant. Hikaru said Eveline's group was doomed for failure and I had no reason to believe he lied. At least, not at the time."

Mike chose that moment to walk into the kitchen. He held an empty plate and glass. His hunger still hadn't diminished since his teenager years. He placed the dirty dishes in the sink, probably assuming the magical dish fairy would move them to the dishwasher for him.

Knowing Mom, he wasn't wrong.

"I found something," Mike said.

"Sunshine69 is Mrs. Baker from Juni's house fire case?" Raven batted her eyelashes for additional theatrical effect.

Mike's mouth fell open. He took a second to collect his thoughts and then leaned forward, bracing his hands against the kitchen counter. "How?"

"Sometimes strong detective work doesn't require technology, just good deductive reasoning." She tapped her temple.

"Juni recognized the email address, didn't she?" Mike raised an eyebrow.

"Yeah," she admitted.

"So, the next question is why Inari kept tabs. Did she want to prevent the tethering from happening?" Juni asked. "Feed them false information?"

"Or did she want to aid them?" Mike added. "Using Hikaru to give them helpful information?"

"And guide them to her domain for the tethering, most likely claiming some crap story of how her court would provide better access to the Realm of Light," Juni said.

"Oh, she's in this deep." Raven pushed away from the dining table. "That's why she wouldn't answer my questions when we visited her. She wants the Lighters to succeed so she'll get all the tethered souls as indentured servants."

Her siblings looked over at her—Mike with impatience and Juni with raised eyebrows.

"That's why Bane wanted my help," Raven said, the information clicking into place. The back of her neck prickled as her brain raced through all the possible outcomes. "He doesn't need assistance smiting some ignorant regs. Though he took a calculated risk, he could've whisked his son away to safety at any time. He did all of this to manipulate me into agreeing to that deal. He knew a god from the Realm of Light was involved."

"He might be powerful, but even the mighty Lord of War can't take on a god," Mike said. "He's either setting you to act as his shield or to take the fall."

It didn't sound any better when Mike said it than it did when it was a fledgling, unspoken thought in her head.

CHAPTER 27

"Things don't get easier, you get better."

— AUTUMN CALABRESE

R aven stepped from the *seomra cumhachta*, the special power-boosting room in her Corvid Court fortress. Instead of feeling drained from checking in with the barrier, her body hummed with energy. That room was better than a spa.

She walked along the stone corridor, dreading the next part of the day. Rourke fell in line behind her, somehow emerging from the shadows as if he were made from them. If Raven didn't know better, she'd assume he was, but shadows weren't Rourke's power. As a weapon warper, he excelled with all things pointy. With his aim almost guaranteed and the ability to fashion anything into a weapon, Rourke had a successful career as an assassin before he tied his life to Raven's.

If his pointed teeth didn't give him away as a killer, the way he moved would. With strong muscles, relaxed posture and a centred way of walking, he moved like a fighter.

Cole moved in a similar way.

Maybe it was a dark fae thing. She hadn't met a single one that didn't exude some sort of deadly purpose.

Huh.

No wonder Lloth underestimated her. Compared to everyone surrounding the former Queen of Corvids, Raven would've appeared weak and inexperienced. Which she was. Then and now, but inexperience didn't mean she couldn't learn and improve, and that was what Raven spent all her spare time doing. She took years mastering the scythe she now carried, years practicing how to speak fae just to gain a basic understanding of the difficult language, how to use fae politics to her advantage and to avoid bloodshed, how to rule a shadow kingdom and how to wield her powers effectively.

Maybe they should change the family motto to something like, "Things don't get easier, we get better."

She heard that once from one of her friend Megan's workout videos.

Raven paused and shook her head. Scrap that. "Everything is better with bacon" was more fitting and already the well-established family motto.

"Are you feeling okay?" Rourke asked.

"All this stuff with Juni and now my great-grand-mother is emotionally taxing," she admitted. She wanted a spa day.

Maybe a spa month.

Rourke had stepped up to walk beside her, no longer trailing her like a living shadow. She hated when he did that and it took her years to break him of the habit.

As she spoke, Rourke scrunched up his face. "I wasn't asking about your feelings. I meant physically. You look pale and you're walking stiffly."

"I'm pretty sure Mike tried to poison me."

"Again? Didn't you learn the last time with the meat pies?" he asked.

"Apparently not."

Rourke visibly mulled the situation over and shrugged. "You probably deserved it."

"Ha, ha." She hadn't lied to Cole when she told him she didn't want to hang out in the same space as Rourke and Mike. Those two were merciless together and inevitably the discussion would turn to her incompetence or questionable life choices.

Rourke smiled, large enough to show off his pointy

teeth, before his expression turned serious. "Our bond feels weird. You feel weird."

"Back off. I'm stressed, okay? Not weird." She sent the scythe away so she didn't hug it through the courtyard. "And those chips really did make me sick."

Rourke grumbled but walked in silence beside her. When they entered the courtyard, Bane was already waiting for them. His long, black cape whispered against the black stone flooring. He tapped his armoured boots with impatience.

Her sentinels lined the aisle on both sides, alert and wary of their guest.

"Have you been waiting long?" Raven asked sweetly. Today she wore the female version of Cole's fae armour. Now that she knew how to sift objects through the shadows and combine it with her ability to portal or shift, she had no need to wear the battle bikini unless she wanted to. It had many advantages, but today, she was cold. The black matte metal absorbed the light instead of reflecting it and though she wasn't as lethal as Cole, at least she emulated the dangerous vibe.

"You know I have," Bane snarled at her question.

"We've been a bit busy." Understatement of the year. She refused to apologize for his inconvenience. The Lord of War had been inconveniencing her since the first day they met. It was time he managed his expectations.

"Nice armour." Bane scanned her outfit with his

stony expression. Was he sincere or mocking her? Hard to tell.

And she didn't care.

She widened her smile and sat on her throne of metal feathers. With a wave of her hand, she granted permission for Bane to approach and the sentinels stepped out of the way.

"You can leave us," she told the guards. Rourke already knew her well enough to know she excluded him from that order. He'd ignore her anyway if she told him to leave.

Her caomhnóir stood behind her and slightly to her left. His hands didn't drift to his daggers like the fae equivalent of a gunslinger in a western, but he managed to make a minor shift in his posture to immediately change his bearing from casual to deadly.

"You're here so we can discuss our plan." Raven forced the tension from her shoulders and clasped her armrests.

"I thought we'd have some tea and discuss the weather." Bane said. "Marvelous day we're having, isn't it?"

Raven snorted. "Having tea with you is a visual I could do without."

"I can be very civil when I need to be. I have a lot to offer."

"I'm sure the only two things you have to offer are dick and disappointment," she said. "I'm not interested in either. I have a plan for the Lighters. Would you like to hear it?"

Bane looked stunned for the first time since she met him. He snapped his mouth shut and glared. Minutes passed while he sorted through whatever raced around in his calculating mind. "I don't care for whatever cockamamie shit you've strung together," he finally said, drawing himself up as if his full fae armour and huge stature would intimidate her. "I'm here to tell you what you're going to do."

Not today, Satan.

"Is that so?" She leaned back in her throne. "You must have me confused with one of your servants."

"I'm not confused, I'm asserting my dominance."

"Last time you tried that, you lost."

He growled.

"Have you been hanging out with werewolves? Fae tend to use words for communication."

"Are you trying to piss me off?"

"Not particularly." She shrugged. "It's just an added bonus."

Bane took a deep breath. "You are so tedious. Cole must've lost his mind."

"Only his heart," Raven said. "And if you expected me to cower before you like a weakling, you're the one with the lost mind. You took advantage of my sister's vulnerability and bound her to you for all eternity. Did you really expect me to roll out the welcome mat?"

"I helped her unlock her divinity so she could save

her lover boy. Juni isn't weak or helpless. She's skilled at using a variety of weapons, has politically significant ties and was trained by the best weapon warper in the Underworld. I don't see what I did wrong. If you're expecting special treatment, you're sitting on the wrong kind of chair."

"My sister is twenty-one years old. She might be an adult in the Mortal Realm and have enough sass to take on an entire battalion of soldiers, but she's still very naïve about the world. Something you're well aware of. You saw a weakness, an opening, and you exploited it. You can do us both a favour and just admit it instead of trying to excuse it."

"I'm not denying anything," Bane snapped. "Besides. Juniper would've had a great career as my caomhnóir."

She cocked her head. "Did your mom not hug you enough as a child?"

"My mother was ripped apart on the battlefield by my father so he could wrench me from her womb."

Raven recoiled.

"So I guess not."

She hesitated. Bane showed no softness, no inflection of emotion, but his words cut through the silence of the courtyard.

"Did…" She hesitated again. "Do you want a hug?"

Odin's balls, please say no.

"Fuck, no," Bane said.

Hallelujah.

"Look." She leaned forward and continued as if she hadn't just offered to comfort the Lord of War. "We need to work together to make the best plan for success. Why don't we push all this personal stuff to the side? You tell me your plan, I'll tell you my plan, and we'll see what we're working with."

Bane sneered, curling his upper lip back to reveal his perfect teeth. "Fine."

Fine. She just negotiated a temporary truce with the Lord of War. What in the Underworld was the world coming to?

"What's your plan?" she asked as if the words didn't slice her to pieces. Ugh. Being considerate to Bane physically hurt.

"We obliterate every Lighter stronghold we find." Bane shrugged as if the idea of killing potentially hundreds of roller-loving people who were completely innocent of wrongdoing was of no consequence.

Well, duh.

Lord of *War*.

"Or..." Raven waited for Bane to stop glaring. When he didn't, she continued anyway. "We use your son as bait."

He blinked at her. "Have you lost your mind?"

She waved his comments away. "Let me finish. What if it's not actually your son? What if we make them think we have your son to hand over?"

Bane's frown deepened. "Glamour? If they're roller groupies, they might have charms and wards to see through such deception. We'd only have one shot at this, and that's a gamble I'm not willing to take."

She shook her head. "I'm thinking of something better than glamour."

"Like what?"

"A chameleon."

CHAPTER 28

"I was going to take over the world, but then I saw something shiny."

— UNKNOWN, BUT ALSO RAVEN

It took every ounce of Raven's dwindling self-control not to punch Mr. Christian Smith in the throat. The so-called father had grasped his "son" in a suffocating hug while he cried fake tears. Dressed in a light blue sweater over a collared shirt and designer jeans, he looked like the cover model for some parenting magazine. But Raven knew the truth and this man did not deserve to parent.

"Thank you so much." Christian wiped a tear from his cheek and held the chameleon against his body.

The "boy" turned so they could see his profile and winked.

Raven sighed. The bait and switch had worked. "I'm glad this story had a happy ending."

The chameleon had readily agreed to help, citing the need for fresh air. Iashi hadn't been concerned about Salril's promise to assist but was extremely annoyed Raven hadn't made any progress on the missing troll case. Raven didn't blame her. Lack of progress annoyed Raven as well but walking into Inari's domain right now was a terrible idea, especially considering they suspected her involvement with the Lighters.

The missing troll would be her number one priority after this case closed. She'd already arranged a messenger to travel to Inari's court in the morning.

Raven held out a form on a clipboard to Christian. "I know this is not the best timing, but we need to discuss the final payment."

Christian looked up and narrowed his eyes. He kept his arm around the chameleon, locking him in place. "Right now?"

"Yes." Normally, they'd record the hand over and set up an appointment for a later date to sign off on all the final paperwork, but they wanted this case officially closed and paid before Christian got what he absolutely one hundred percent deserved.

"What of my ex-wife?"

"What of her?"

"Is she alive?"

Raven jerked back. "We're not assassins, Mr. Smith. Your ex is most likely wandering around the forest looking for your son. We'll provide the police with the location once we're done here."

His frown smoothed out. "Which is why you want to settle now. You're worried I'll try to back out of the payment once the police apprehend my ex."

It seemed Christian understood asshole behaviour quite well, which said a lot about him. A lot they already knew. In reality, they had recourse as a business with a signed contract. They could take Christian to court if he tried to refuse or fight the final payment. Court took time, money and posed a small risk of loss, but that wasn't why they sought immediate payment. If everything went well, Christian wouldn't be around long enough to make it to court. Bane had called dibs, and no one bothered to argue with him. Christian would get what he deserved.

Christian thanked her for the millionth time before signing the form that acknowledged acceptance of the final bill for the case, granting them permission to charge his card on file. Normally, Raven and her family had more tact than billing a distraught parent on site, and this grated her nerves, even though there were extenuating circumstances and Christian didn't deserve any gracious behaviour.

Along with Kayden's shorts and shirt, Salril was outfitted with a long-range tracker. He'd also granted

Raven permission to carry some of his blood in case they needed to relocate to him. The chameleon seemed unconcerned about the unknowns in the case and the potential dangers. Raven had been very clear they couldn't account for every possibility and couldn't guarantee his safety one hundred percent.

Salril didn't care. He practically bubbled with excitement.

Raven learned long ago not to bother questioning Others. They all had an arsenal of special skills and the more dangerous ones kept their secrets close.

The chameleon needed a mere five minutes in Kayden's presence to imitate his appearance to perfection, as well as his speech patterns and mannerisms. The chameleon was good. She couldn't detect any differences.

After saying goodbye to the Worst Father of the Year, Raven walked to the car and slipped into the passenger seat. Cole sat behind the wheel while Rourke and Bane sat shoulder to shoulder in the back. They all wore regular mortal clothing, but the shirts and jeans did little to camouflage their Otherness.

Cole's eyes widened at her once she returned. He looked weird. She scrunched her face and opened the bond.

Ah.

He felt awkward.

That made sense given the tension coming from the backseat. Raven turned to the two men. They looked like sardines stuffed in a can. Despite the back-seat technically being a three-seater, their wide shoulders pressed together. They looked squished and uncomfortable. "Did you two kiss and make up?"

"Interesting choice of words," Cole muttered.

Now she really wanted to know what went down while she made the exchange.

Rourke scowled at her and Bane merely smirked. Maybe he made that face to cover discomfort. Maybe it wasn't just arrogance.

"Anyone want to tell me why it feels so Odin-loving uncomfortable in here?" she asked.

"Nope." Cole reached forward and turned the car on.

"Never," Rourke said at the same time.

Bane continued to smirk. He had such a smarmy face.

"Whatever." She turned back to the front, pulled her phone out, and called Mike.

He picked up on the first ring. "Tracking is initiated."

"Perfect. I'll open the app once I get off this call. Are you guys ready to follow?" she asked.

"Yeah..." Mike's voice came out a little higher pitched than normal.

"Why do you sound weird?" Geez. Tonight was not the night. What was wrong with everyone? Then her memory flipped through all the recent events and she let her irritation go. A lot had transpired in the last few weeks. Maybe the Crawfords had finally found their quota for the amount of crap they could handle in a certain chunk of time.

"Do we have to bring them?" he whispered.

"Hey!" Juni growled somewhere near him and a thud followed the sound of her voice.

Mike grunted.

Either Juni or Lincoln must've hit Mike. They were all in the car together, but given Juni's fiery temper, Raven would bet her battle bra their sister was the one to throw the punch.

"We're not sure what to expect or if we'll have to follow multiple targets. Having extra shifters will come in handy." She explained. "But remember—I don't want you engaging unless absolutely necessary."

"Yeah. Okay," Mike said.

"I mean it."

"Uh-huh."

She frowned at her phone. "You know all this already. Why are you questioning the plan now?"

"It's just...uh. You wouldn't understand the level of awkward being stuck in the car with these two."

Raven glanced over her shoulder at the two men behind her. "Oh, I think I have an idea."

She hung up before she had to listen to more sibling rivalry and pulled up the tracking app. The direction of the blinking dot surprised her.

Cole watched expectantly.

"They're not heading to Eveline Baker's house."

Not unless they planned to take the most roundabout way there. The red dot zoomed by the turnoff to Christian's house. "And he's not taking the kid home."

Rourke leaned forward to look at the screen over her shoulder. "Looks like they're heading out of town."

Raven nodded. "Bad Dad isn't wasting any time."

Bane growled in the backseat. Actually physically growled like he was some sort of wild animal. She understood the source of his anger. If they hadn't intervened...If the mom hadn't taken Kayden...If Christian actually had the real Kayden in his possession...this would've been the fate of Bane's son.

"He's safe," she reminded him. The last thing any of them needed right now was a raging Lord of War in the backseat of the car.

His lip curled up in a cruel snarl. "I know."

Raven glanced at the screen again. "He's taking the Number One out of town."

"Got it." Cole indicated and changed lanes to get on the on-ramp. Someone honked. Repeatedly.

Cole smiled, and she suppressed a groan. She knew that grin. That grin said he wanted to fight. Any slight, any perceived threat, any smidge of a reason, he'd unleash. The boys in the back made him feel uncomfortable and now he wanted to vent.

Bane wore an almost identical smile.

If Raven were the praying type, she'd slap her hands together so fast right now and pray for the driver behind them to let go of their road rage. They had no idea that fae-packaged rage filled this car.

Cole gripped the steering wheel and kept alternating between looking at the road ahead and the rear-view mirror. His smiting smile grew.

Oh dear.

She reached out and rested her hand on his forearm. Though the tension remained in Cole's grip and tight expression, the bond between them relaxed a little.

The car behind them honked again, pulling right up to the rear bumper.

"Let me out," Bane growled.

"Absolutely not," Raven said. "We need to keep moving. That driver is inconsequential."

"You made me stay in the car while that pathetic norm who wants to murder children took my son's doppelganger."

Right. Bane wanted to smash stuff, too.

The driver behind them honked again, swerving their vehicle side to side. The lane beside them was clear. The driver could go around. Instead, they clearly wanted Cole's attention, which meant they'd probably continue their antics.

She winced. This wouldn't end well.

"What if they're involved?" Cole indicated and pulled the vehicle over.

"They're not involved. They're just another

Vancouver driver with a bad case of lane entitlement and road rage."

He shook his head and shoved the gear into park.

"I agree with Camhanaich. We need to investigate." Bane's expression remained emotionless.

Cole winked at her. "I'll be right back."

All three men exited the vehicle.

Why was this her life?

Unfortunately, the guy in the other car didn't develop any common sense or self-preservation. He'd also pulled off the road to park behind them. The dark fae men stood and waited as a large reg, with traps bigger than his head, stepped out of the sleek sports car. Underneath a fitted tracksuit that looked ready to rip at the seams, he wore one of those tank tops that showed off his muscles. One slight twist and he'd serve them with an unsolicited nip-slip. The track pants were too tight around the thighs and tapered to the ankles, and the bright white of his sneakers indicated he rarely wore them outside.

"You cut me off," the man snarled.

Seriously? All this anger for changing lanes? This guy had lost more time with his antics than the few seconds it took to let Cole into his lane.

The men didn't respond.

Rourke shifted position and suddenly the man was splayed against his vehicle's hood, tacked in place with ninja stars through the jacket's collar. Rourke had somehow spotted the only free fabric on the guy's entire outfit, aimed, and threw his ninja stars. And he did it all within a split second. Her guardian was so badass.

Bane and Cole both glared at the weapon warper. He'd stolen their fun.

Completely unaffected, Rourke looked over at them and shrugged. "We needed to speed this up."

Cole's shadows whipped out from the embankment and surrounding area and wound around the man. The man's eyes widened.

In the meantime, Bane called his broadsword to him. Much like how Raven called her scythe, one moment Bane stood emptyhanded, and the next he held a massive weapon. Rage ripped around the dark fae lord, and his sword dripped blood, screaming for more. Legend had it the blood held the essence of all his victims and the screaming came from the last sounds they made before he ended their lives.

"Who sent you?" Cole asked, his voice deceptively light.

"S...sent me?" The man's gaze flicked back and forth, panic creasing his expression. "Nobody sent me. You...you cut me off."

In unison, the anger drained from the fae men. Their shoulders relaxed and they glanced at each other.

That's right boys, you attacked a weak reg whose only crime was being an idiot armed with a horn.

Cole had the audacity to look sheepish as he turned to her. "I guess you were right."

"Of course, I am. Now get back in the car." She pointed at the vehicle just in case they needed clarification. "We have some real business to attend to."

Bane and Cole sighed, stalking back toward her.

"Rourke?" She placed her hand on her hip. What in the Underworld was her caomhnóir doing now?

"What?" Leaning over the man, he paused to look back at her. "They're good weapons."

He wrenched a ninja star from the car. Metal groaned but gave way. He held it up to the sunlight, rotating it back and forth to check for damage before making it disappear in his armour.

Odin save her from weapon-loving weapon-warpers. She got back in the car and waited for her guardian to retrieve the rest of his ninja stars.

CHAPTER 29

"Oooo. Shiny."

— EVERY SINGLE ONE OF
RAVEN'S BIRDS, FFS

Transforming into a conspiracy of ravens, most of Raven's birds perched on branches around the parked car while they waited for her siblings to get into position on the other side of Whitehead Park. Even though they had to park by the side of the road outside the park's entrance to remain undetected, the tracker confirmed Christian had gone inside the park with the chameleon.

Raven focused her attention on the bird currently resting on Cole's shoulders. She'd already sent a few birds ahead to keep watch on Bad Dad and the chameleon. They were also waiting in a car.

Lots of waiting.

Lots of boredom.

Lots of shiny litter to distract her conspiracy.

"They're in position." Cole held up his phone so the bird on his shoulder could see the text from Lincoln. She butted her bead against his cheek. He reached up and scratched behind her ears.

Ohhhhhh...

That felt nice.

Though avian species lacked the external pinnae humans had, they still possessed internal cochlea. Instead of a spiral shape, though, it's mostly straight and it felt so good to get scratched right behind them.

Ahhhhh...

"Raven." Rourke's flat voice held exasperation and a reprimand all at once.

She used the bird perched on his shoulder to gently jab his cheek with its long beak.

"Piss off." He flicked his hand at the bird's face before rubbing his cheek.

She ignored her whining guardian and launched the remaining birds to spread them out and take positions around Christian.

Bad Dad had moved, taking his son along a path until they reached a lookout.

The area was quite beautiful. Tall evergreens swayed in the gentle night wind. Old stonework paths and lookout areas lined the cliff's edge and provided mountain views and sightlines to Horseshoe Bay during the day.

Raven moved the conspiracy, bird by bird, until she had a raven at each vantage point while the rest stayed out of sight within the surrounding trees.

"Where are we going, Dad?" the chameleon asked, eyes wide.

Odin's shriveled berries, that entity could win an Oscar.

"Shh..." Christian patted the boy's shoulder absentmindedly as he continued to lead him to the edge of the lookout area. He still had his arm draped around the child's shoulders. To onlookers, he might appear like a doting father, but to Raven, he looked nervous. He looked as though he worried the boy would flee and mess things up. The arm kept Kayden close and provided Christian with a sense of control.

"I want to go home," the chameleon said, wrapping his arms around himself.

"This won't take long. Then we'll go and I'll get you one of those kid's meals you like so much."

The boy's gaze brightened, lighting up his whole face. "Promise?"

"Promise." Christian ruffled the boy's hair.

Christian Smith was a lying piece of shit. Anger boiled in her veins. The urge to pull her magic, reform in front of this vile human being and hurt him raged through her entire being. She fought the compulsion.

She pushed the anger down. She couldn't lose control of her conspiracy right now. Not when they were so close to discovering the driving force behind this venture.

The bird nearest to the father and son croaked and hopped on the low branch.

"Fuck." Christian jumped back.

"What is it?" Salril asked.

"That's the biggest fucking crow I've ever seen."

Hah! Crow. If Raven could roll her bird eyes, she would.

"You shouldn't say those bad words," Salril said.

The wind picked up and the trees swayed. The air around the father and son swirled, faster and faster, cutting off what Christian said. A portal of blizzard-like crystalline flakes snapped in place. The portal wasn't actually snow, no matter how much it resembled the stuff.

Dread clamped her little bird brains. This was not a development she wanted. Sure, she anticipated Inari's involvement. They all did. The kami already had an agent in the roller groupies. But keeping an eye on some regs and being actively involved in potential child-murder were two completely different things.

Inari, in her striking woman form, stepped from the portal and validated the dread rattling through Raven's conspiracy.

Behind her, Chad stepped from the portal, hauling a young troll child with him. Chad Berkley lived beside her parents' house. At one time, they assumed Chad was just some clothes-hating reg who had a habit of walking onto his balcony naked. It wasn't until Raven broke into his home that they discovered he was a light fae lord sent to watch over the Crawfords on Inari's order.

Oooo. Shiny. One of Raven's birds zeroed in on the troll youth.

The young troll had stubby horns and a chubby face and wore a necklace with a triangular pendant.

Her raven croaked, wanting to get closer, wanting to snatch the jewelry away. Raven focused on the shiny metal. The troll wore the same pendant as Iashi and King Tethaahin. The one with the rune for loyalty etched into the metal.

Well, then. Looked like she found the missing troll prince. She'd only have to face off her great-grand-mother, who happened to be a light fae *god* to get him back.

Did they plan to sacrifice Prince Tuguh as well?

And how on earth would three shifters, two dark fae lords, a weapon warper and a reg confront her great-grandmother?

The bird ruffled its feathers, as if to stay warm, when really, the swarm of emotions unsettled it. Another one of her ravens moved to a closer branch, wanting to see the shiny thing, too. Its wingbeats echoed against the stonework—*whoosh, whoosh, whoosh.*

Inari considered Christian and the boy as the portal snapped shut behind her.

"This is most unfortunate." Inari's silken voice broke the deafening silence.

Christian straightened and clutched Kayden closer. "What do you mean?"

"We can't do the ritual." She narrowed her eyes and peeled her pouty lips back to reveal perfect pearly white teeth.

Pretty sure that smile would beat Cole's smiting smile on the scary scale.

"Why not?" Christian asked. His grip tightened, bunching up Kayden's shirt. "I've done everything you asked. You promised to do the ritual tonight if I brought my child."

"Yes, but..." Inari jerked her chin toward the chameleon. "That's not your child."

The chameleon remained frozen where he stood, pressed against his fake father's side.

"Of course, he's not my child," Christian spat. "That's the whole point, isn't it? He's some dark fae lord's bastard. You need one of fae blood and one of the jotun." He waved his hand frantically at the troll child and the chameleon. "You have what you need."

Raven paused and waited. No roaring. Either Bane kept himself in control or he was too far away to hear the remark.

Whew.

Why would Inari snatch the troll prince? Did the

ceremony require noble blood? Surely any other jotun would've been easier to snatch than the prince. It had to be his royal blood.

"Not your child. Not a dark fae lord's child, either." Inari's scary smile widened as she blinked at Christian. "Oh, no, silly mortal." She raised her arm to point a dainty finger at the chameleon. "That's not a child at all."

CHAPTER 30

"A child shouldn't have to pay for the sins of the parent."

— RAVEN CRAWFORD

A number of things happened at once. Raven gathered her energy and reformed in the lookout area in her full fae armour with her skull-emblazoned scythe in hand. Cole and Bane stepped from the shadows of the nearby walkway where Cole had been shielding them, and the chameleon embraced his true form.

Christian Smith squealed and jerked away from Salril.

"I never could fool you," Salril said.

Christian scrambled backward to escape, his eyes so wide they looked as though they'd pop out of his skull at any moment.

Inari spared Salril a small smile. "It's been a long time, Sal. I'd ask you who you were acting on behalf of, but my great-granddaughter's dramatic entrance has already answered that question."

Raven didn't want to have the evil villain conversation. She wrenched on her power and Cole's through the anam cara bond and lashed out. Bands of shadow whipped around Inari, wrapping her tightly in shadows.

"You were going to sacrifice young children," Raven said.

Inari turned her cool gaze to Raven. "I was going to break the chains you have placed on us. Two deaths are a drop in the pail compared to war," Inari said.

"You'd go to war with me?"

Inari scanned her again, posture relaxed, expression neutral. "Not at the moment, no."

In the periphery of Raven's vision, Christian inched away from the clearing.

Raven tightened the power around Inari and glanced at Chad to ensure he didn't try anything. With Bane and Cole standing a few feet away, she doubted he'd lift a finger.

Bane finally turned to Christian when he made it halfway to the treeline, rage washing off him in waves. "You're not going anywhere."

Christian froze.

Raven considered the situation with Inari. She didn't like the direction of her thoughts but ruling in the Court of Corvids had taught her she sometimes had to make tough decisions to protect those she cared for.

"Maybe we only need one death to stop a war," she mused. She'd already discarded the idea but wanted to gauge the light fae's reaction.

Inari snorted. "If you planned to kill me, you would've already tried."

Tried. Interesting. Maybe Raven didn't have the power to kill a god. She had yet to really test her limits, but now didn't seem like the time.

"You will let us go." Though Chad spoke with a calm voice, his tense shoulders and stiff lips said he didn't have as much faith in Raven's motives as her great-grandmother.

The troll child watched the exchange, his intellect clear in his black gaze as he inched away from the light fae lord in tiny steps.

"Why would I do that?" Raven asked.

"You owe me."

"How is letting my great-grandmother go so she can start a war even payment for breaking into your fake home?" she asked.

"Make it even." Chad folded his arms across his chest.

Checkmate.

"You will leave the troll child with us. When I release Inari, she will not retaliate. You will not retaliate. You have safe passage into your portal, and you will swear not to harm, imprison or attack us in any way."

"My sweet summer child," Inari said. "Why would I hurt you?"

Huh?

"Do you honestly think you have the skill or luck to wrap me in your borrowed magic? That I would just stand here without recourse. These bands cannot contain me for long, nor do you have the power to destroy me."

Well, now that she mentioned it, the whole thing did seem rather easy. Raven lowered her scythe and glanced at Cole. Her husband shrugged.

"Then why did you let me wrap you up?" Raven asked Inari.

The kami smiled. Not the creepy smiting smile this time, but a wide, genuine one. A smile that would make anyone fall to their knees and worship her.

"I would never needlessly jeopardize my line, nor the continuation of it." Inari dropped her gaze.

Raven followed her gaze. Why in the Underworld would Inari look at her stomach?

Oh.

OH.

The scythe slipped from her fingers. Before it clattered to the ground, she caught the weapon with her magic and called it back to her hand.

"Raven?" Cole asked, alarm streaking through their bond.

She so did not have the time to process this.

"Release Inari." Chad interrupted what should've been a special moment between her and Cole. "We agree to your terms for this evening and this evening alone."

"I swear." Inari held her hand up in the air. The smirk returned and it reminded her of Bear.

"I'm pregnant?" She didn't feel pregnant. She'd know something like that, wouldn't she? She couldn't be pregnant. She didn't want to be pregnant...right? What in the Underworld was going on? Inari must be mistaken.

And if Inari wasn't? Why had no one said anything? Though the fae wouldn't have sensed anything, the skulk of foxes that made up the bulk of her family certainly could.

Instead of dwelling on the torrent of feelings, she withdrew the magic wrapped around Inari. The goddess stepped from the falling magic, brushing the shadows aside like dust in the air. She walked across the stones and stopped in front of Raven to place her delicate hand over Raven's stomach. The kami's hand was surprisingly warm and contrasted with the coldness in her black gaze.

"I'm not willing to risk this branch of the family

tree," Inari said. "Not yet. Not when things have started to get interesting. I want to see where this story goes, though it's vain of me to do so. But never forget. That's exactly what you are to me. A branch. One of many. I will not hesitate to cut one rotten line to save the tree."

Message received. Inari wasn't above smiting them all if they became too much of a nuisance.

Inari withdrew her hand. Neither Inari nor Chad said another word as they walked into a new portal and disappeared. The fragrant petal smell clinging to the air faded away.

The chameleon held the troll child, like a mother comforting her own. Hopefully, Salril would see the prince safely back to the trolls' domain while she got her mind under control from all the reeling.

Bane looked bored, but he'd subtly moved closer to the man who would've sacrificed his child.

Her siblings and Lincoln were nowhere in sight and Cole...

Cole looked gobsmacked. He stood with his shadows curling around him, the moonlight playing with the harsh angles of his face. His eyes had bled out, all black, as intense emotion rocked him.

They'd been together over six years now and shared an unbreakable bond, yet seldom had she seen this expression on him. Vulnerable.

"A baby?" he whispered. Fae children were rare. It took couples decades, sometimes centuries to conceive.

"Yeah, I'm out." Bane grabbed Christian and threw a lodestone down. Christian screamed for help, thrashing against Bane's tight hold.

Bad Dad's cries didn't faze Raven at all. He would've killed a child, a child he helped raise for years. She could understand his anger when he discovered the truth, but that wasn't Kayden's fault. The child shouldn't have to pay for what his mother did.

"Congratulations," Bane threw over his shoulder before he disappeared into the angry red haze, carrying the other man's screams with him.

Cole ignored the fading dark fae power from Bane's portal and waited for her response.

Could she be pregnant? Inari didn't seem like the type to lie. Maybe her upset stomach hadn't been solely from the physical excursion, heat, and bad chips. She shrugged, helplessly. "I guess? I didn't know."

"I did," a husky woman's voice crooned from behind Raven. At the same time, two arms wrapped around her body, snuffing out Raven's power on contact.

"No!" Cole lashed out with his magic.

The woman jerked back, dragging Raven with her while her dark energy soaked into Raven's skin and prevented her from transforming.

A black portal snapped shut around them.

The last thing Raven saw was the look of fury on Cole's face and his shadows not reaching her in time.

"Now we have some time to chat, woman to woman."

Raven finally placed the voice and dread clamped her body all over again.

Nyx.

CHAPTER 31

"She's the light in my otherwise dark existence."

— COLE CAMHANAICH

The moment Raven pushed free from Nyx's grip, she spun around and lashed out with the shadows. Power ripped from her body.

Nyx laughed as the magic crashed against a shield and fell away like breaking storm waves on a rocky cliff face.

Nyx.

Nyx and Erebus were in Chaos' first batch of children. Said to be born from the primeval void, they became primordial gods. Legends claimed Erebus' dark mists spread over all the realms and filled every crevice within, while Nyx, the Goddess of Night, gathered Erebus' darkness to create night.

Erebus was also Cole's father, which made Nyx Cole's aunt by blood and evil stepmother by marriage. Yeah, the relationship was exactly as it sounded —twisted.

To make it more complicated, Nyx hated Cole. He represented Erebus' infidelity and love for another woman. It wasn't enough for Nyx to orchestrate the death of Cole's mother, she also made it her life's side mission to make Cole and Chloe miserable. Another jilted lover taking out the parent's sins on the child.

Now, she'd kidnapped Raven—Cole's pregnant wife and anam cara. Raven hadn't had time to process the whole pregnancy thing, but one thing was abundantly clear to her—Nyx had the ability to devastate and break Cole with one fell stroke.

Raven had trained a lot since she met Cole. She knew how to wield her power, how to embrace her strengths and shield her weaknesses, but against a goddess? Nyx?

"I don't wish to fight," Nyx called out from behind her protective shield.

Nyx, dressed entirely in black, radiated magic in waves. With dark hair and dark eyes, the tall woman with a lithe build perpetually wore a haughty expression while somehow managing to give "dangerous" a whole new look.

But apparently, Nyx didn't want to fight.

Yeah, like that put Raven at ease.

"Let me guess," Raven said. "You just want my firstborn child?"

Nyx cackled. She said something else, but Raven missed it. Instead, she reached out with her magic and probed the shield. Her power brushed against a wall made entirely of dark energy.

Raven refused to stand there as a target for Nyx to practice on. Nor would she let Nyx do whatever she had planned. At least not without a fight. Raven might have misgivings about her impending motherhood, but she wouldn't fail to protect her unborn child and her husband.

The shield might repel any magical attack, but would it block her physically? Raven glanced around the room. She stood in the centre of a dark space with no apparent exit. Stone made up the ground and the four walls. Above, a ceiling of jagged rock, preventing an aerial escape. Glowing material covered the rocks and provided the only source of light. The hazy blue glow pulsed.

Raven called her magic to form a portal. At least, she tried to. Her magic wouldn't obey the command.

She tried again.

Nothing.

She still had magic. The power pulsed under her skin, ready to use, but wielding her magic against Nyx while she stood on the other side of that shield was futile and a waste of energy.

Raven growled and turned back to Nyx.

The goddess watched her, arms folded across her chest. "Are you done trying to find a way out?"

Nope.

"Are you ready to talk, yet?" Nyx's seductive voice filled the room.

Definitely not.

Mom spent the better portion of her childhood reminding them about the dangers of making deals with fae. Raven had ignored the advice at almost the first opportunity, in favour of Cole's dark, brooding looks and his promise to keep her family safe. Luckily for Raven, that deal turned out successful, but her life experiences in dealing with the fae had taught her the validity of Mom's lessons. Cole and Rourke excluded, of course.

"Let's save some time, shall we. You can't portal out, and your magic won't penetrate this barrier. Let's talk and make a deal," Nyx said.

Still not liking that option.

Nyx said her magic couldn't penetrate the barrier. The goddess mentioned nothing about physical objects. Raven lifted her scythe, holding it across her body with both hands and ran at the barrier.

Nyx's eyes widened.

Raven slammed through the shield. It scalded her skin, like it stripped off the outer layer. She made it through and barrelled into Nyx.

The goddess smirked, breaking her fall, and rolling

effortlessly with their momentum. Before Raven had a chance to orient herself, Nyx's boots planted into her stomach and pushed her away.

Raven sailed through the air. Her scythe flew out of her grip and soared across the room to clatter against the cold stone floor. Before impact, she willed the change, splintering into a conspiracy of ravens only to reform in front of Nyx. She drew her fist back and punched Nyx. Her fist slammed into the goddess' face. Pain raced up her arm from her knuckles. Nyx's head snapped to the side, but she didn't fall. She didn't even stagger and Raven hit her with everything she had.

Instead, the goddess wiped the blood from her nose and smiled. "Saucy wench. I see why Cole likes you."

Raven stepped away in time to miss the initial attack. Quick and vicious, Nyx lashed out. Raven blocked the blows and reeled backward. With a frenzy of strikes, she had no time to think, only to react. Nyx hadn't drawn her dagger.

Why hadn't the goddess slit her throat when she first had the chance?

Attack after attack, Nyx drove her back. A few shots snuck through Raven's guard. Pain ached in her ribs from a jab and her jaw throbbed from a mean elbow.

Nyx caught her arm and jumped up, un-expectantly. The goddess swung her leg around before gravity and her own body weight had them both crashing to the floor.

Raven tried to roll. She tried to push away.

Nyx wrapped her legs and arms around her.

Raven couldn't move.

Panic set in.

She thrashed.

"Shh," Nyx whispered. "You fought valiantly for such a youngling. I'm impressed. If you survive your first century on your throne, you'll be a force to reckon with."

Raven continued to fight against the hold.

"Stay still. This won't take long."

The magical shield dropped, and Nyx's dark magic swept in to curl around Raven.

"No!" Raven writhed in the other woman's hold and watched helplessly as the magic pooled around her stomach.

Around her baby.

"Consider this an early baby shower gift," Nyx hissed.

Raven screamed. She tried to pull on her power. Nyx's contact with her skin fizzled out her corvid essence.

Nyx's magic sunk in and...

And stopped.

The potent power collided with an invisible shield.

Raven dug deep, pushed past the barrier Nyx's touch created, pulled on the shadows from her bond with Cole and wedged her power between her and the goddess. She tore free from Nyx's hold.

"How is that possible?" Nyx barked. "Why would the wild magic of the jotun protect you?"

Raven didn't have the answer for Nyx, but she said a silent thank you to Vel'am from Torghatten all the same.

"Guess it just likes me?" Raven gathered her magic, preparing to form a shield and find a way out of this place before Nyx came up with a plan B.

"No matter," Nyx spat and unsheathed her dagger. "I will deliver my gift another way."

Before the Goddess of Night took another step toward her, the air vibrated with rage. A seam in reality ripped open. Shadows flowed from the tear, revealing Cole at the centre. His eyes had bled out, all black, but the transformation didn't stop there. Shadows had consumed his skin, giving him a dark gray complexion. He looked like wrath personified and vibrated where he stood a few feet away.

Nyx said something, but Raven missed it. How could she hear anything else over Cole? He roared, a deep, dark scream of fury. It shook the ground beneath them. Nyx had stolen his pregnant mate and he had come to reap vengeance. He'd torn through whatever magical defenses Nyx had used to secure this place. He wasn't angry.

He was furious.

Power emanated from his skin, bathing her in waves of magic. The potency burned, like sitting too close to a bonfire. Cole never claimed to be a hero, and she wasn't naïve enough to believe he was. He wouldn't sacrifice everything and everyone to save the world and do the righteous thing.

No, not Cole. He'd burn everything down to save her.

Shadows wrapped around Nyx and pinned her to the nearby wall. They continued to layer over each other. Shadow band after shadow band until only Nyx's strained face remained visible.

Cole held her in place a foot off the ground, strangling her with her own body weight. The pale pallor of Nyx's cheeks grew redder and redder. She opened her mouth to gasp for breath.

"Can't..." she bit out. "Kill...Me."

Cole's smile was terrifying.

"Oh, I can, but I won't resign either of us to the grave just yet." Cole squeezed his power, pulling on Raven's through the bond. "I can, however, make you wish I did."

A shiver coursed up Raven's spine. She somehow managed to place one foot in front of the other to stand beside her husband.

The redness of Nyx's face faded away. "You're such a drama queen."

"No." Cole stepped toward her and squeezed his power some more. "I'm the Lord of Shadows, but I could be King of the Night."

Nyx sneered.

"I ripped pieces from the Realm of Light and the

Underworld to create a refuge away from you and your games. I could break my promise to my father and rip you apart, too, consequences be damned."

"You wouldn't dare."

Cole's skin darkened and rage continued to vibrate through their bond. "If you took from me the one light in my otherwise dark existence, I'd have nothing else to lose. I'd take my revenge and then I'd gladly face the consequences. Never forget that, Nyx. I can and will kill you if you ever harm Raven. That's my promise to you."

The goddess' expression closed off, all smirks and sneers gone. "Don't worry, youngling. I never forget anything."

Yeah, that didn't sound ominous. Not at all.

Cole wrapped Nyx in more shadows before turning to Raven. His gaze gleamed, wild and fierce. He gripped both her arms and pulled her into the heat of his body. He crashed his mouth against hers, hard and claiming. It was not a gentle kiss. It was possessive. It was angry. It was fear and relief at the same time. But most of all, it was love.

And she drank it up as if her life depended on it, because in a way, it did.

EPILOGUE

"The most dangerous woman of all is the one who refuses to rely on your sword to save her because she carries her own."

— R.H. SIN

"I still can't believe you let that crazy bitch go." Juni scrunched up her face from where she sat across the dining table from Raven.

Honestly, Raven would take that expression—the one where Juni looked as though she just smelled wilted spinach—over the heated glances her sister kept sending the man sitting beside her. If Juni kept looking at Lincoln like he was a plate of bacon, they'd all have to leave a perfectly good Sunday Roast Night to give them privacy.

"I had no choice," Cole said. "Not unless I wanted to start a war with my father or submit to the punishment for breaking a fae oath."

"What exactly did you promise him?" Dad asked, momentarily forgetting the roast beef in front of him. Raven heard his unspoken questions. What promise was more important than protecting his daughter? A bit unfair seeing how Cole had spent almost every minute since he met her finding ways to ensure her safety.

"When I created the Shadow realm, my father realized the extent of my power. We are evenly matched. I may not win if I challenge him, especially if Nyx joins in, but Erebus realized his own victory wasn't assured. He promised not to retaliate for what I did if I promised not to kill Nyx." Cole's expression and the anger pulsing through their shared bond said how much he wished to break that promise.

Raven made no such promises.

"So while her life is safe from me," Cole continued. "Mine is not safe from her."

"And your father isn't safe from you," Mike noted.

"My father and I have a complicated relationship, but I don't wish him dead," Cole said. "Besides, killing Erebus wouldn't help the situation. A dark fae promise sworn on an oath rope transcends death." He paused, his scowl deepening. "I looked for a long time for any loophole."

"What exactly would happen if you broke the promise?" Lincoln asked.

"I will suffer a most horrific death."

"Can't you just keep her in that prison of yours?" Mom asked. "Or have Raven do the actual killing?"

Thanks, Mom. Just sign me up for some assassination. No biggie.

"Father would go to war with us. I want Nyx to pay for what she did and for what she keeps trying to do, but a war against the Realm of Night and his legion of dark soldiers will not give us that. It will only give us death."

Honestly, a war right now was something none of them needed. Raven still had a whole bunch of crap on her plate. She had to fulfill her promise to Bane to take out the Lighters, because she wasn't naïve enough to believe Bane getting Christian was enough to meet the terms of the agreement. Inari could still be an issue. Would the kami leave Raven and her family alone, or would she try some other devious way to destroy Raven's barrier? And then they had their own family dynamics to discuss. Mike, Juni and Mom needed to discover the full extent of their powers, and no one had addressed the large elephant in the room—Dad didn't have any light fae powers.

Had no one else realized the ramifications of that? Or were they willfully ignoring it like she tried to do?

The thought...the idea...ugh. It hurt so much she didn't want to think about it at all.

Mom tapped her fingers along the table. "What exactly did Nyx do to Raven?"

Everyone turned to her. With a heaping fork of mashed potatoes half-raised to her mouth, Raven froze before slowly setting her cutlery down. "We don't know. Somehow the wild magic from Torghatten cloaked me from her magic. She wasn't happy about it. We don't know what Nyx planned to do or whether she was only partially or fully prevented from carrying it out."

Raven glanced down at her flat stomach. She didn't feel pregnant yet, but four pee sticks confirmed Inari's proclamation. When would the motherly feelings kick in? When would she feel pregnant? Right now, she felt as she always had, but everyone around her had already started to treat her differently. Like she was fragile and incompetent. Mom even offered to come over and clean.

Mom hated cleaning.

Though excitement trilled in her veins, she also worried about the changes this baby would make in her life. Yes, most would be good, but if her own family had begun to see her as something different, what did that mean for the fae? Would they perceive her as weak? Would they use her own child against her? Would they wait for the birth, or would they start plotting against her the moment they found out about the pregnancy?

Would this make her weaker? Would she be more vulnerable? Would bursting into the conspiracy harm the baby? Had she already hurt her unborn child?

Sweet baby Odin.

She'd transformed into her conspiracy countless of times over the last week alone. Her hand slipped to her stomach and she swallowed the guilt already threatening to rise and consume her. She couldn't undo the past. Every fox nose in this room confirmed she was still with child.

Every. Single. Fox. Nose.

"Thanks for the heads up, by the way." Raven couldn't decide who to glare at, so she settled on Mike. He'd been by her side a lot these last few days and in his fox form. He had to have picked up the change in her scent. "Pretty odd that a whole skulk of foxes missed the pregnancy hormones in the air."

Mike jerked his head back as if she slapped him. "At least I kept gum with me. I read mint was good for settling stomachs. Besides, what the fuck was I gonna say? You obviously had no clue or were purposefully not saying anything. Given your history, I banked on you being clueless. It's not for me to break that news for you. Not when you're about to visit your great-grandmother for the first time or when you're tracking down lost children. Nor is it an easy thing to drop into normal conversation."

"So I ran the usual background checks on our client, but found nothing." Juni chimed in with a fake deep voice, obviously impersonating Mike. "And congrats on getting knocked up."

Rourke choked on his potatoes.

Raven reached over and slapped him on the back a couple of times.

"I don't sound like that." Mike frowned at Juni before turning back to Raven. "I honestly thought you'd figure it out after all that puking."

"What puking?" Cole glowered. "You told me you felt fine."

"Easy." Raven shot her youngest brother a glare before turning to her husband. "Don't break out the bubble wrap just yet. I feel fine."

He narrowed his eyes at her.

"Now," she clarified. "I feel fine *now*."

Juni leaned forward and pointed her fork at Raven. "So if it's a girl, will her first or middle name be Juniper?"

Lincoln snorted.

Mom groaned.

"Please just promise us you won't refer to it as crotchfruit," Rourke said around a mouthful of food.

The rest of the dinner conversation devolved into a conversation of potential baby names, each suggestion more ridiculous than the last. Raven leaned back and let the sounds of her family's witty banter wash over her. She enjoyed this time. Them.

Her hand slid over her stomach again and a pang of

worry spread through her veins. What exactly had Nyx planned? Had she harmed the baby in any way?

Even if the goddess was ultimately unsuccessful, it left another rather distressing question. What in Odin's pink pickle had Vel'am done to her and Cole's unborn child? No one had asked her that question yet, and for that, she was grateful.

In the end, it wouldn't matter. It didn't matter. She held her still-flat stomach and made a silent promise to her unborn child. Though she hadn't planned for this, she would be strong for her baby. Fierce. She wouldn't rely on others to shield her. Cole would protect her and the child ferociously, but she wouldn't look to her knight in shadow armour at every hint of danger. Protection was her jam. She'd look for her own scythe and if she had to, she'd cut down the whole world if it meant keeping her dark legacy safe.

~The End~

Want to know what happens to the
Crawfords next?
Look out for *Outfoxed*
(*A Raven Crawford Sibling Story*)
due out Winter 2021

If you haven't read the Juni Crawford books yet
and want to know more of her story,
start with *From the Shadows* (A Crawford
Investigations Story, Book 5)

GLOSSARY OF TERMS & CHARACTERS

Allfather: Odin, ruler of the Underworld. Raven's maternal grandfather.

Anam cara: Dark fae term that roughly translates to "soul friend." This is an eternal fae bond that allows two souls to flow together allowing the bonded fae to access each other's strength, power, and magic.

Bane: Dark fae lord. Also known as Luke Bane. Lord of War.

Bhanrigh: Dark fae for "queen."

Bear Crawford: Caller of Corvids. Raven's twin. Married to Chloe.

Caomhnóir: Pronounced "keevenoyr." A guardian blood sworn to protect fae nobility.

Chad Berkley: Light fae lord. The Crawford's neighbour. Also known as Tarzan.

Chloe Crawford: (née Camhanaich): The Claíomh Solais. Cole's twin sister and Bear's wife.

Christian Smith: Kayden Smith's father.

Cole Camhanaich: Full fae name is Beul na h-Oidhche gu Camhanaich (pronounced: Bee-al nuh huhee-khye guh Ca-van-eekh). Raven's husband and anam cara. Patron Fae of Assassins and Lord of Shadows, Son of Erebus born of Chaos.

Dark fae: Any fae from any of the realms within the Underworld.

Eveline Baker: Roller groupie.

Felicia Johnson: Kayden Smith's mother.

Finna: Dark fae sentinel.

Gwawrddur: Troll who tried to force Raven to act in the interests of the jotun.

Hikaru: Kitsune from the Realm of Light.

Hōju: A golden orb said to grant wishes in a time of need. Gifted to Juni from Inari.

Iashindinn "Iashi" Kanwann: Troll ambassador.

Inari: Japanese kami of grains, harvest, and agriculture. Juni's maternal great-grandmother. She/her. He/him. They/Their.

Joseph Beauchamp: SPOILER. (not telling you. Nee-ner, nee-ner, nee-ner).

Jotun: Trolls.

Juniper "Juni" Crawford: Fox shifter. The youngest of the Crawford siblings. Juni took over Crawford Investigations with Mike after their father retired.

Lighters: An organization comprised of roller groupies who are obsessed with the Realm of Light.

Lincoln: reg. Former classmate of Juni's and former prisoner in Raven's dungeons. Imprisoned for his part in Juni's abduction by a hyena shifter gang.

Marcus: Witch. Bear's best friend.

Mike Crawford: Raven's youngest brother. Hacker, programmer, technology extraordinaire.

Mo bhanrigh: Dark fae for "my queen."

Mortal: Any inhabitant of the Mortal Realm. Note: All entities of all the realms can be killed, but this term is reserved for anyone who is not an Other. Used as a derogatory slur by Others.

Nerthach: Troll who tried to force Raven to act in the interests of the jotun.

Other: Any inhabitant NOT from the Mortal Realm. Any inhabitant from the Realm of Light, the Underworld or the Shadow Realm. Mortal, but not a mortal.

Reg: A "regular" human being from the Mortal Realm without any supernatural powers or skills.

Regulators: An organized group of regs who despise Others and hold meetings to bitch about the unfairness of life.

ROL: Realm of Light. An Other realm full of rollers who look down on everyone else.

Rollers: Supernatural beings from the Realm of Light.

Rourke: Dark fae weapon-warper. Former member of Assassin's guild. Currently, Raven's life-bound guardian.

Salril: Chameleon.

Seomra Cumhachta: Dark fae term that roughly translates to "room of power." This room maximizes a magic wielders power by taking advantage of the natural environment and the infrastructure to align magical elements.

Tethaahin: King of the trolls.

Three-P (3P): Permanent personal portal.

Torghatten: A collective term to refer to all the troll tunnels. Also a mountain on Torget Island in Norway.

Tuguh: Troll prince.

Underworld: An Other realm, often in direct conflict with the Realm of Light. Contains multiple, smaller realms, such as the realms of War and Lust.

Vel'am: honorary name for the wild magic of the jotun.

VIN: Vehicle Identification Number.

ACKNOWLEDGMENTS

I'd like to thank the usual suspects: WP, NF and KB for their beta reading prowess, Anna from Eerilyfair Designs for the gorgeous cover, Lara Parker for the editing and Book Nook Nuts for the proofreading. Any errors in this book are mine and mine alone, despite their attempts to help me.

And finally, a huge thank you to my support network—my family, friends, and my lovely readers. Thank you for putting up with my Canadian spelling and grammar. Thank you for the reviews and the messages. And thank you most of all for reading my books.

ABOUT THE AUTHOR

J. C. McKenzie is a book loving, gumboot-wearing, unapologetic science geek. She predominantly writes urban fantasy and post-apocalyptic dystopian fantasy with strong romantic elements. When she's not spinning tales, she's in the classroom sharing her passion for science and mathematics while secretly warping the young impressionable minds of our future to carry out her evil plans for world domination. She lives in the Pacific Northwest with her family.

Visit her at jcmckenzie.ca

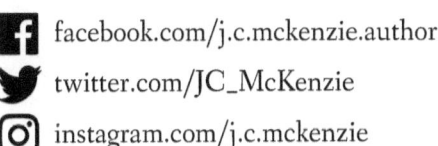

facebook.com/j.c.mckenzie.author
twitter.com/JC_McKenzie
instagram.com/j.c.mckenzie